FINALLY YOURS

ELENA AITKEN

Also by Elena Aitken

Finally Series

Finally Yours

Finally Mine

Finally Fell

Finally Forever

Finally Free

Bears of Grizzly Ridge

His to Protect

His to Seduce

His to Claim

Hers to Take

His to Defend

His to Tame

His to Seek

Hers for the Season

Bears of Grizzly Ridge: Books 1-4

Bears of Grizzly Ridge: Books 5-8

Ever After

Choosing Happily Ever After

Needing Happily Ever After

Wanting Happily Ever After

Second Glances

Winter's Burn

Midnight Springs

She's Making A List

Summit of Desire

Summit of Seduction

Summit of Passion

Fighting For Forever

The Springs Collection: Volume 1

The Springs Collection: Volume 2

The Springs Collection: Volume 3

The Springs Complete Collection - Books 1-10

Timber Creek

When We Left

When We Were Us

When We Began

When We Fell

Timber Creek: The Complete Series

The McCormicks

Love in the Moment

Only for a Moment

One more Moment

In this Moment

From this Moment

Our Perfect Moment

Chapter One

THERE WAS NO WAY.

Absolutely no way.

It didn't matter how many times I stared at the number, it didn't get any smaller.

As if that would matter.

Even if it got smaller, I'd still be screwed.

But still.

I clicked on my phone one more time in case there'd been some sort of miracle, and scrolled through the email that had come through from the college admissions office one more time.

Yup. Still screwed.

$11,000.

For *one* semester.

Well, maybe it wasn't quite eleven thousand. I was rounding up. But only by a few dollars. Not enough to make any real difference. Either way, the number still made me sick to my stomach. How could they get away with charging so much for college classes? Was it even legal? Did it even matter?

It didn't, because I needed those classes to finish the college degree I should have finished years ago. The real question was, where the hell was I going to come up with that kind of money to pay my tuition?

So much for bettering myself.

So much for trying to start a whole new life after my husband of over fifteen years proved to not only be a philandering asshole, but also a cheat and a fraudster, too.

I really needed to stop being so shocked by it every time I thought of it. It was pathetic and I may be a lot of things, but *pathetic* was not and would never be one of them.

All the signs that Daniel was a dishonest swindler siphoning millions of dollars from his client's investments had been there for most of our marriage. I'd simply chosen to ignore them. Just as I'd chosen to ignore his string of girlfriends for the last ten years or so. It was easier not to rock the boat. Fortunately, it didn't make me complicit in the crime. Just an idiot.

An idiot who, at forty-one, was trying—and clearly failing —to start over her life.

How could anyone start their life over when the only job you could get without a college degree in the upscale town of Aspen Valley was minimum wage, which barely paid for rent and food? Never mind trying to afford anything extra, like the education I should have pursued instead of marrying Daniel and falling into a life of luxury that turned out to be based on nothing more than lies.

I wasn't usually such a negative person, but it was starting to look more and more hopeless. Since I had to declare bankruptcy because of Daniel, there was zero hope of getting a loan. Hell, I was lucky I even got a job. Apparently being married to a douchebag who'd swindled millions and claiming ignorance about it all didn't make you seem very credible *or* smart.

Not that getting the job in the pro shop at the Aspen Valley

Country Club I used to be a member at was very lucky. Far from it.

Serving the men and women who used to call themselves my *friends* was—

"Excuse me?"

Speak of the devils.

Bitsy Neville and Janine Lister, two of the women who I'd spent countless hours shopping and lunching with in my former life—my stomach turned just thinking about how I'd become such a shallow version of myself while I was with Daniel—flitted into the pro shop.

Bitsy's gaze zeroed in on me. She raised one heavily penciled eyebrow and pursed her lips together. "Isn't there a club policy about employees using their cell phones during working hours?" She made a clicking sound with her tongue and wagged her finger, as if I were a child.

I swallowed hard.

You need this job. You need this job.

"We wouldn't want management to hear about this, now would we?"

You need this job.

"After all," Bitsy continued, a sour grin taking shape on her overly made-up face, "club members are the most important thing, aren't they?"

I could say a lot of things about what was really impor-tant, but I didn't. My mantra still rang through my head. I *did* need the job. As demeaning as it was. Every penny counted.

"I'm so sorry, Mrs. Neville." I tried not to choke on the formal way I addressed her. Club policy. "What can I help you with today? Is there something specific you're looking for?" My voice dripped with fake sincerity, not that I expected her to notice. And she didn't.

Instead, she flipped her hair over her shoulder and shrugged. "No. I'm just browsing today."

"Of course." I nodded demurely. "You just let me know if—"

"You should probably put that away now." She nodded to my cell phone, still in my hand. "I would hate to see you reported, after all."

"Of course." Dutifully, I tucked my phone away under Bitsy's watchful stare.

Satisfied, she spun on her heel and wandered around the shop, picking things up, carrying them around, and then purposely putting them down again where they didn't belong.

You need this job.

Although I was fairly certain the job had only been given to me to humiliate me and make the other members feel better about themselves. Sadly, most of these people enjoyed treating me like a piece of shit on the bottom of their overpriced designer golf shoes a little too much.

Still. It was the only job I had. It was a paycheck and I'd take it. At least until I could finish up my degree and get a real job.

If I could find the rest of the money I needed for the final semester. I had vastly underestimated how much tuition prices had gone up since the last time I'd taken a class. Not for the first time, I was kicking myself for not just finishing my degree while I had a chance. Marriage could have waited a few more months. In hindsight, it could have waited a lot longer than that. Like, forever. But, hey…there was no turning back time now

At any rate, I almost had all the money I needed. *Almost.*

I had some from my grandmother's inheritance when she passed a few years ago that the banks couldn't touch when they came collecting. The classes were paid for. Mostly. The books for those classes were another thing altogether. Over a thousand dollars for *books?* It was robbery. Especially considering most of those books were delivered digitally. How was I supposed to study from my phone? I realized I was showing my age, but I couldn't help it. I wanted to pull out an old-fashioned highlighter and a packet of sticky notes like the old days. And if I was going to have to sell a vital organ in order to pay for those books was it too much to ask to actually *have* the books?

And it was looking like I might have to if I didn't come up with a solution, and soon.

I took a breath, exhaled slowly, and scanned the shop. I tried to ignore the stacks of sweaters that Bitsy had very clearly tousled and the shelves of boutique lotions that were no longer neatly lined up with the labels facing outward. I'd fix that later.

My eyes landed on Janine Lister, who was trying on shoes. No doubt she *did* need assistance if she was trying to shove those size ten feet of hers into a size eight golf shoe. I rolled my eyes. For as long as I'd known Janine—a long time—she always insisted she wasn't a size ten.

To hell she wasn't.

I shook my head, but didn't bother going over to offer help because even if I offered it, I knew from past experience she wouldn't take it. Instead, she'd stick up her nose and make some kind of snide comment about my clothes or my car or... well, any other insult she'd probably spent the night before thinking up.

As terrible as Bitsy had been, Janine seemed to have made it her personal mission to try to make me feel as worthless as she possibly could. Just the way she used to spend all of her time sucking up to me. But that was when my husband was one of the club's most influential members.

Her two faces were just about as overpowering as the scent of her flowery perfume that probably cost more than my paycheck that filled my senses a few minutes later when she wandered up to the till with a box of the size eight shoes in her hand.

Janine never did know when too much was too much.

It made my stomach roil to think that I used to be friends with these women. Not that you could ever really be friends with stuck-up, snobby socialites. For the millionth time in the last few months, I was grateful I'd maintained my friendships with my *real* friends. Women who'd been by your side since you were thirteen and knew everything about you, and loved you despite it, were worth their weight in gold.

"Did you find everything you were looking for, Mrs. Lister?" *Rules were rules.* "These are a nice choice," I continued before she could say anything. "And an eight. I'm so glad we had your size in stock." I smiled. If she'd been paying any attention at all, she could see how fake it was.

Fortunately for me, unless they were actively insulting me, none of them paid me any attention. Not now. Now I was a nothing. This time last year, she would have been kissing my ass because of who I was married to. It was such bullshit. So fake.

How quickly things changed. And those changes were not necessarily all bad. Not at all.

"I'll wear them at the charity event next week."

Janine was talking. I nodded and smiled as if I cared at all. She handed me two hundred-dollar bills to pay for shoes that were one hundred ten and didn't even bother looking at the change before she stuffed it in her Gucci wallet.

It would have been *so* easy to short her. She'd never notice a few dollars missing, and maybe I could at least pay for my—

No, Abby! I chastised myself while at the same time putting on a bright smile for her. "I hope they bring you luck."

Because your game is terrible.

Fortunately, Janine was too dumb, or too oblivious, to

notice my jab. I held my fake smile until Bitsy rejoined her and together they left the shop. As soon as they were gone, I sagged against the counter.

Fuck. Double fuck.

I could not start stealing. I was *not* Daniel. I was absolutely *not* my husband.

Ex-husband, I quickly corrected myself.

No. I had morals. Daniel didn't even know what they were. But…fuck morals. I needed the cash. Besides, this was different. Daniel took money from the rich and *kept* it. I would be taking money from the rich and giving it to the poor. Me! That was different. And I was just as much a victim of Daniel's crimes as everyone else.

Okay. Maybe not.

But still. Was it fair that I was left to piece my life back together when all of Daniel's *victims* barely even noticed a few dollars missing from their own bulging bank accounts?

No.

But it was too much of a stretch. I was desperate. But not *that* desperate. *Yet.*

I gave myself a nice little pep talk and did my best to put my money troubles out of my mind. At least for a few minutes. I focused on stocking the shelves and changing out displays until my shift was over and I could go home to my tiny apartment.

I was standing on a step stool, doing my best to reach for the bust of a mannequin dummy that needed a fresh shirt display, when I heard *his* gruff, rough voice.

"You should be careful up there. It's not safe to stand on a ladder without someone spotting you."

I spooked and lost my footing a little, causing the ladder beneath me to wobble. To my horror, I shrieked like a little girl but then quickly found my footing a moment later when the ladder stabilized. And that's when I finally dared to look.

I knew the voice.

I knew it very, *very* well.

And I knew damn well what was attached to that voice. Which was why I both didn't want to look and also, more than anything, did.

I squeezed my eyes shut for another second, took a breath in an effort to compose myself, and finally looked down to see Phillip Conrad.

The Phillip Conrad.

Phillip was a ridiculously handsome man, built like a Greek god, with a full head of thick dark hair streaked with silver, and just a bit of stubble—that was new—on his incredibly chiseled jaw. Somehow, while most of the men in Aspen Valley got soft around the middle and had hairlines that moved farther back on their foreheads, Phillip did the exact opposite and just got more handsome. If it were possible.

And apparently it was.

Just like everyone else at the club, we used to be friends. Only Phillip had been more than a friend. A *lot* more. He'd been…well, we'd dated a long time ago. Before Daniel. I'd *really* liked him. I mean, *really* liked him. The kind of like that you might even call…*love*. At least you might call it that under different circumstances. *Very* different circumstances.

But that was all ancient history, because then I'd met Daniel. And even though I was dating Phillip at the time, as soon as Daniel came along, it was as though Phillip suddenly lost interest in me. As if I didn't even exist. One minute, I thought we were getting serious and ready to take our relationship to the next level, and the next minute…it was over. It left my head spinning. Fortunately—or not, in hindsight—I had Daniel to distract me.

But that didn't mean I'd stopped thinking about Phillip. Not at all. For a while, I'd tried to talk to him about *us*. But I had my pride and it didn't take long to figure out that he wasn't interested in whatever I thought we'd had. So, I moved on. Mostly. After a while, it was just easier to go out of my way to avoid him. It sure as hell hurt less if I didn't have to see him. Because no matter how much time passed, every time he looked at me with those dark eyes, it did something to my insides.

And now, here he was. Standing directly beneath me, one hand on each arm of the ladder, his face pointed up—giving him a fantastic view up my short khaki uniform skirt at my—*oh shit*. I was in desperate need of doing laundry, but the shoebox I was renting didn't have machines and I hadn't had time to go to the laundromat and—I'd gone commando.

The blush in my cheeks came hard and fast. I grabbed the mannequin with one hand for balance and quickly made my way to the safety of the solid floor. "Thanks."

He grunted in acceptance but didn't move away, leaving me boxed in between the ladder and his hard chest. He was taller than me, at least six two, with a wide, broad chest, and thick, muscular arms that—despite the fact that he probably thought I was a *nothing* just like everyone else—sent a thrill through me, right between my legs. Something about a big, strong man never failed to turn me on.

No. Correct that. Something about *Phillip* never failed to turn me on. Not that I'd admit it. Especially not now. And especially not with his dark eyes and the way they were staring at me that would have definitely made my panties wet—had I been wearing them.

"You shouldn't be putting yourself in danger like that."

He looked at me with a disapproving smirk on his face.

"I'm fine."

"But you might not have been."

"Right." I tried to slip away, but his arm didn't move. "Excuse me."

My body trembled, and I hoped like hell it didn't show.

I had no right to let myself feel anything around this man. Although it had been *him*, not me, who'd lost interest in our relationship. I thought we were going to...it didn't matter. Once Daniel came home from Europe, and I met him for the first time, everything changed. He'd pursued me intensely and Phillip...he'd just backed off, as if I hadn't meant anything.

And maybe I hadn't.

But maybe if he'd called again, asked me out one more time...maybe I wouldn't have married Daniel.

Yes. I knew that was true.

I'd liked Phillip *a lot* more than Daniel. I'd been completely turned inside out with him. I would have done anything for him, and our attraction to each other was off the charts. So I'd thought. But it had never gotten physical. He said he wanted to wait, and I'd agreed because I didn't want to mess it up by sleeping with him too soon. But then again, maybe that's why he was able to walk away so easily? I still wondered about that. Like Phillip was the one that...what? Not got away. But the one that filled my thoughts. That I thought about. And fantasized about. All. The. Time.

"I mean it, Abigail. You could have been hurt."

I paused and looked at him suspiciously, just the way I looked at anyone in this place who said more than two words to me. Let alone anyone who showed any concern at all about me.

"Of course, Phill—I mean, Mr. Conrad." I caught myself and the stupid rule of employees not calling the members by their first names. Talk about degrading.

For a minute I thought he might correct me and ask me to

call him by his given name. Instead, he nodded and said, "Mr. Conrad? Hmm…"

I couldn't even begin to explain why such a simple comment turned me on the way it did.

I needed to stop thinking of him like that. After all, not only was he a member, he was *Phillip Conrad*. Perhaps one of the most important, and wealthiest, members of the club. And there was too much history between us for it ever to be anything else. And that's exactly how I should be thinking of him. In fact, it was the *only* way I should be thinking of him.

"Yes, Mr. Conrad." I nodded as demurely as I could. "You're absolutely right. Next time I'll have someone hold the ladder."

He eyed me for a moment. If it had been any other time, I would have been absolutely sure there was desire in his eyes. Just when I was starting to think I should go back to work, he took off his suit jacket and handed it to me. "I forgot to return this to the restaurant," he said. "It's a ridiculous dress code. You'd think since I spend thousands of dollars here every bloody day that they'd let it slide."

"Rules are rules," I said, just the way I was supposed to, even though I agreed with him. Phillip Conrad was known to routinely tip extravagant amounts in the bar and restaurant. If only I could get transferred there and away from the stupid pro shop, a lot of my troubles would be over. At least financially. I'd have a whole host of new problems actually *serving* my former friends. Still.

I took the jacket from him and laid it over my arm. "I'll return it right away, Mr. Conrad."

For a moment, I thought he might say something else. His lips turned up in a very slight, very sexy grin. "It was good to see you, Abigail." And then he nodded before he turned to leave.

I watched him walk away. No, I watched his firm ass as he walked away. *Damn.*

As soon as he left the shop, I let out a breath I didn't even know I'd been holding and returned to the till to find something to occupy my time until I could close up. The sooner I could put Phillip and his ass out of my mind, the better I'd be. I needed to focus, and not on the *one who got away.*

I'd return the coat on my way out. The restaurant had a ton of loaner coats for guests who forgot the dress code or, like Phillip, just refused to comply. They wouldn't miss this one for another hour or so. I tossed the coat up on the counter and something fell out of the pocket.

Oh.

Phillip's money clip.

He must have forgotten it. I picked up the thick stack of bills. And holy shit was it thick. There must have been thousands of dollars there. I flicked through it quickly, mentally adding up the numbers.

"Oh my God."

I counted again. Slower this time.

Twenty thousand dollars. And he'd just forgotten it, as if it were nothing.

What was clearly pocket change to that man could have paid for two whole semesters of my college education.

Or maybe only a few bills could pay for my books?

The idea was intoxicating.

And so very, very wrong.

Morals. Remember?

Still.

It's not as if Phillip would miss it, and it would be a life changer for me. I'd be able to breathe again. I wouldn't have to drop out of school. Really, it would be an act of charity.

Only the donor would never know.

Not that it mattered.

I fingered the bills again, and before I could chicken out, peeled off a few of them and stuffed them into the only place I could think of—my bra.

Holy shit! What had I just done?

No way had I just done that.

If anyone found out, it could cost me my job. Hell, I could go to jail. It could cost me *everything.* Just like it had Daniel. But…it was just so easy.

And nobody would get hurt. Phillip was richer than God. And he… He wouldn't—

A hand clamped around my arm like a vise and a familiar rough voice rumbled through me. "What in the hell do you think you're doing?"

———

I'd gotten all the way to the car before I realized I'd left my billfold in the pocket of that stupid jacket. Shit, Abigail Blakely —I mentally used her maiden name—she had me *completely* distracted. Just the way she always had. And that was *before* I'd had a look up that sexy little skirt the club made her wear.

Did she even know she wasn't wearing panties?

Of course she knew.

I'd seen the flush on her cheeks.

Damn.

I blew out a breath, slammed the door of my car, and turned back to retrieve my money clip, and I sure was glad I did. Because not only did going back give me another chance to see Abigail—and I'd take as many chances as I could get— but as it turned out, I was treated to a whole different kind of show.

Abigail didn't see me watching as the money clip fell out

onto the floor. She didn't notice me when she picked it up and started flipping through the bills. She wasn't paying any attention when her eyes grew wide and then even wider as she realized exactly what she was holding.

Twenty thousand, five hundred and twenty-two dollars.

You didn't get to my position in life without knowing exactly how much money you had at any given time.

It wasn't any secret that Abigail Blakely was broke. Worse. She was broke and humiliated. Maybe it should have surprised me to find out that Daniel had been arrested for embezzlement and fraud. But it didn't. He always had been the snaky sort. Point in case, he'd gone after and *taken* Abigail right out from under me all those years ago. Just the way he'd always taken everything else he'd ever wanted. As if Abigail could ever be *taken*. No. She was so much stronger than that. It was only one of the reasons I was surprised she hadn't seen right through what a douche Daniel was back then, or any of the years in between. I almost stepped in when she agreed to marry him. *Almost.* But what would I have said? *Don't do it? You deserve better?*

Yes. I could have said any of those things. But like a fool, or a chicken shit, I'd kept my mouth shut. Maybe it had taken years, but at least she'd finally seen the truth about Daniel now.

Not that she had any other choice when the authorities burst into their home, dragged her husband out, and confiscated pretty much everything they owned. It would be pretty hard to miss the truth then.

Still, watching Abigail look at my money clip the way she was, as if it were food and she were starving, tugged at something deep down in my core. Or was it a different kind of hunger she stared at that money with? Her breath came faster and harder, her polo straining and pulling against her breasts with every breath.

It was probably just my imagination. Lord knew that when it came to Abigail, my imagination knew no limits.

I could have watched her all day. Although, as it was, my dick throbbed painfully, needing release. Abigail always did have that effect on me. It was why I'd tried to stay away over the years. Distance was the only way I could manage not being with her.

It was why I needed to *get* away then and why I needed to get away now.

Just as soon as I got my money clip back.

I was about to set foot into the pro shop and do just that when, out of nowhere, right there out in the open, in front of what probably were security cameras tucked in the corner, and directly in my own line of sight, Abigail peeled off at least five bills and shoved them in her bra like it was nothing.

Fuck.

I knew she needed the money. How could she not?

But to take it? That wasn't the Abigail I knew. She must be more desperate than I thought. The thought of it caused me physical pain.

I couldn't be sure how much she'd taken, but it didn't matter. I didn't need it.

But she did.

And just like that, I had a choice.

I didn't have to say anything. In fact, it would have been a whole fuck of a lot easier for me to turn the other way and pretend I hadn't seen a damn thing. And really, what did I care if Abigail took a few dollars? I certainly wouldn't miss it. Sometimes I felt I *owed* it to her in a weird, twisted way for introducing her to Daniel. Besides, if she got caught, it was her ass on the line, not mine.

Her ass.

Damn. Her ass was like a ripe peach in that snug, short skirt.

It was that ass that had caught my eye over fifteen years ago, too. And like a magnet, it was once again her ass that had attracted me into the pro shop in the first place. I'd just happened to glance in the shop on my way out, and caught a glimpse of those curves I would know anywhere. *Abigail.* Normally, I would have dumped the loaner jacket with the doorman, but it gave me a good excuse to get a close-up look at her, her still luscious breasts, and—who was I kidding—to talk to her. Because that's what I really wanted to do.

Sure, it was her ass that caught my eye. But it was every other single thing about her that held it.

So with the opportunity to talk to her right in front of me, I'd be a fool to pass it up. And I was a lot of things, but a fool was most certainly not one of them.

Which was exactly why, instead of turning around and walking right back outside, or even pretending I didn't see anything when I went to reclaim my money clip, I walked right in there and grabbed her arm. "What in the hell do you think you're doing?"

Sure, it would have been easier for me to look the other way, but I'm a smart man, and smart men do not pass on these types of situations. Even if I still had no idea what I was going to do with it.

Besides, it was Abigail. She'd always been feisty, with a strong-willed streak that was sexy as hell, while at the same time also infuriating. Especially once she was no longer mine and the opportunity to tame her wild side was no longer mine. *No.* Not tame. Abigail could never be *tamed.* And thank God for that. I liked her a little wild.

I took a deep breath—forced myself to take a deep breath in order to maintain some semblance of calm and control—and willed my cock to settle down. But the second I looked into her big brown eyes, widened in fright and...*defiance*, it hardened up again.

Fuck.

I was already in over my head. Abigail had an effect on me that clearly hadn't lessened over time. Quite the opposite.

"Phillip...I mean, Mr. Conrad." Her voice shook but to her credit, she didn't cry. Abigail would never cry. Not for something like this.

A pride I had absolutely no right to swelled inside me.

She clamped her teeth together and swallowed hard. "I didn't do—"

"Abigail," I said slowly. "I *saw* you." But that didn't mean I didn't want to see more. Because I did. More than I should. "And you're not going to get away with it."

"No." She squirmed in my grasp, but I held her arm tight. Her eyes flared, and I saw the moment she locked in. Any smidge of fear she had gave way to something else. "You didn't see anything. Because there was nothing to see."

So that was how she was going to play it.

"I may be a few years older, but I'm not blind, Abigail. I saw—"

"Nothing." With a yank, she pulled her arm away and turned her back on me. "You didn't see anything."

Desire flared, hard and fast, inside me. I couldn't tolerate the lie—or the theft—but I had to admire her dedication to it. If it were any other situation, I might have let myself smile. As it was, I had to swallow hard to keep myself focused.

"I should report you." I had *no* idea why I said that. I would never report her. Hell, I didn't even like the management of this pretentious club. The very last thing I'd do was run off and tell them about Abigail's *slip*. Especially considering, no doubt, they'd enjoy it way too much. I hated how everyone at the club treated her just because she had the poor sense to marry an asshole.

But I was stuck. I had to do something. I'd called her out. And I never backed down. All feelings aside, I did have a reputation to protect.

Just as surprised as I was by my declaration, Abigail turned around, shock and maybe even a bit of humor on her face. "You're going to *report* me?"

I crossed my arms over my chest in response.

"I *need* this job, Phillip."

It wasn't lost on me that she'd dropped the formalities.

"You should have thought of that before you took what wasn't yours."

Fuck. *I* hated myself right now. I sounded like a grade-A douche bag. Maybe even worse than the asshole she'd married. But I couldn't make myself stop. Something inside me, deep down, wanted to hear her ask for my help. After all these years, I wanted her to *need* me. And it fucking killed me.

Her breasts strained against her polo again as her breath picked up, and I knew she was starting to panic. Or at least finally starting to worry. Her skin flushed, and I followed the trail of pink down to the V of her shirt where it was unbuttoned just a little too low, the creamy swell of her breast exposed to me. Abigail knew damn well that was against dress code. As was the skirt that was a little too short, riding up those long, lean legs and the complete and total lack of panties.

Again, my cock strained in my pants as my eyes took in all of her. No doubt she knew exactly what I was thinking, too. Well, maybe not. She was probably not thinking about how badly I wanted to pull her up against me so those full, ripe breasts were pressed up against my chest while I wrapped one hand around the back of her head and held her lips to mine as

I kissed her the way I should have kissed her all those years ago instead of letting her walk away.

No.

Abigail was probably not thinking *that*.

She was much more likely thinking that if management knew about the money she'd taken from me *and* the break in dress code, they'd have no choice but to fire her. Even if the decision to hire her had been more about punishing the wife of the man who'd swindled from so many members.

God, I hated this club.

"So?" Abigail challenged after a few moments of charged silence passed between us. "What are you going to do?"

She was doing her best to act brave, but I could see through it. She was scared shitless. Rumor had it she'd gone back to school to finish her degree after all this time. It made me proud. Again, a pride I had no right to feel. Still. I never agreed with her dropping out of school. If she'd been mine—it didn't matter.

What mattered was she was doing it. Where she had found the money for that, I had no idea. College courses had only gotten more expensive over the years, and she'd had a hard time making tuition when we were young. Money would be a problem, definitely. That wasn't a secret. Nor was it a secret that she needed more of it. And she needed this job. Maybe that made me every bit the douche bag I was acting like at the moment, but I couldn't help it.

I opened my mouth to say—what? I wasn't completely sure —when her tongue darted out and licked her bottom lip.

Fuck.

She *was* turned on. At least I thought she was. Maybe it was just the fear of the situation, and what I might do about it. *But*...maybe it was more. Was it me? Did she still have...it didn't matter. My fingers yearned to slide up those smooth, bare legs to dip under that tiny skirt and see if I still had the same effect on her. I didn't need to wonder; I *knew*. Because I knew this woman. I knew her fifteen years ago in so many ways. Even if it wasn't all of the ways I would have liked. Or for as long as I would have liked. Still, I *knew* her.

The flash in her eyes and the flare in her nostrils confirmed it.

"I'll make you a deal," I said before I could stop myself. She crossed her arms over her now heaving bosom, which had the delicious effect of pushing her breasts up and together. No doubt, she knew exactly what she was doing. "I won't say a word about what I saw and you can keep your job."

"If?"

She wasn't stupid. I liked that about her. There was always an *if*.

"If you agree to my conditions."

My mind worked overtime to build those conditions in my head before I said them out loud. But I didn't need to think long. I knew what I wanted. What I've always wanted.

"Conditions?"

Her stubbornness was intoxicating.

"You're mine for the weekend."

Abigail took a step back, her mouth opening in an O as shock registered all over her face. I was certain that even from where I stood, I could smell her desire on the air between us.

"Yours?"

Was it my imagination, or did her voice tremble a little bit?

"There's an event at the club this weekend, and I need a date."

"A date?"

"Are you going to repeat everything I say?"

Her lips pressed into a thin line, but she didn't say no, so I doubled down.

"I need a date, and it will be you. Plus dinner the night before, and breakfast Sunday morning."

Her eyes widened.

"All weekend."

Abigail opened her mouth to object to my little indecent proposal, and I wouldn't have been surprised if she had. Hell, I even surprised myself with my boldness. Still, I did *not* want her to say no, so I delivered my final blow. I knew I was being an ass, but I couldn't stop myself. She always had such an effect on me. "Or I'll report you to management."

Her lips pressed shut again and she squeezed her eyes together, but just for a moment before looking at me again. Her eyes grew dark with what was no doubt a combination of anger and desire. Maybe more anger in this case.

"I'm not a prostitute." Her words were clipped. "I am *not* for sale."

Shit.

I was not trying to imply such a thing. Not at all. But the second I paused long enough to think it through, I could see —*dammit.*

I swallowed hard, but kept my composure. She couldn't say no. I *needed* her to say yes.

"Of course you're not," I said slowly. "And I'm not suggesting anything…" I waved my hand between us lamely. "Just think of it as old friends helping each other out."

Her eyes narrowed, but still, she didn't say no.

"Old friends don't bribe each other."

"Old friends don't steal from each other."

Our eyes locked.

"Think about it," I said after a moment. "I'll be back tomorrow afternoon. I'll expect an answer. Spend the weekend with me, or I report the theft to management."

"I didn't admit to taking anything."

I grinned. "You didn't have to. I know you took it, Abigail."

"It's *Abby.*" She bit her bottom lip and sighed, the first sign of her letting her guard down even a little bit. "What am I supposed to do? Daniel took…well, I don't have to tell you."

Something inside me softened at the show of her vulnerability, but I shook my head. I couldn't lose sight of what I was trying to do. Even if I didn't fully understand it myself yet.

"Tomorrow." I looked her in the eyes so I knew she understood, turned, and walked out.

Chapter Two

"HE SAID, WHAT?" Jessie, one of my very best friends, leaned forward on her elbows across the table. Her mouth fell open as I recounted the story of what I'd done, and what Phillip had suggested, to my girlfriends. We were at *Rosie's Diner*, the little diner on the edge of town that Jessie had bought from the original owner—Rosie—ten years ago when she became a single mom. We tried our best to meet up once a week to catch up on our lives, offer moral support, and more often than not these days, reminisce about the *old* days, when we were in our twenties. Young. Fun. With no responsibilities.

Damn. At just over forty, we were still way too young to feel so damn old. Life wasn't over just because we were a few decades older, right? I mean, fun was still possible after a *certain* age, wasn't it? I'd known these girls since we were thirteen and all ended up in the same homeroom in grade seven. We'd been just as different from each other then as we were now, but we had the common bond of not knowing anyone else and needing allies in a brand-new middle school.

Over the years, we'd seen it all together. First loves, broken hearts, drunken nights in a field, driver's licenses, first jobs, high school graduation, fake IDs, college acceptances, or not, more boyfriends, more broken hearts, marriages, divorces, and everything else in between.

And through all of those important milestones, we'd had fun. Mostly. But I couldn't help but think that the older we got, the less fun we had. Was that because life just got in the way? Or did getting older somehow become synonymous with boring? Did the hot sex, the hookups, the wild adventures all end sometime after your twenties?

It was a thought I'd been having more and more of lately. It was also one of the reasons—okay, the *main* reason—that I hadn't dismissed Phillip's offer right away. Not that I'd told my girlfriends that particular detail yet.

"I say, do it." Brittany Donahue, arguably the most successful out of our group, was a CFO of some sort of tech company that none of us really understood. "I mean, why not? Phillip's hot and you've always kind of had a thing for him, right?"

"I don't know if you'd call it a *thing.*" I picked up my glass and looked into the clear liquid of the martini I'd made myself earlier. It was strong. Very strong. It had to be if I was going to come to grips with the shitshow my life had become.

Yes, I had a *thing* for Phillip Conrad. Although, to say simply that I had a *thing* for Phillip Conrad was a massive understatement. I'd definitely had a thing. A thing that I'd once been positive was love. So much so that I thought that I would marry him instead of his best friend, Daniel. But then he'd let me go. No. He'd practically shoved me toward a relationship with Daniel. Not only did Phillip not fight for me, he walked away from me. And no woman wanted a man who didn't want her. Right?

Hindsight.

"I don't know," Sandy Clark said. The mother of two girls,

and a widow for the last four years, she was definitely the most conservative of our group of friends. I knew she'd be horrified at Phillip's proposal. Sandy sipped at her drink—a coffee with Bailey's—and shook her head. "It sounds kind of—"

"Dirty!" Darla Diamond chimed in.

I knew she'd be on board with Phillip's plan. Single and happily so, Darla had never settled down. She'd spent the last twenty or so years since high school jumping from job to job, and from man to man. And she liked it that way. Frankly, it was exhausting to watch, but Darla seemed to enjoy it. And more than once I'd been jealous of her sexual exploits. Okay, maybe you *could* still have fun after forty. At least, Darla could.

Darla put her whiskey glass on the table and stared into my eyes. "Do it. Why not?"

"I can think of a few reasons."

I actually could only think of one. Well, one that really mattered anyway. Sure, if I went to that party at the club with Phillip, all eyes would be on me. Eyes that used to call themselves my friends. Every single person there would be staring at me, judging me and gossiping about me. But that didn't really bother me. Not really. After all, those people had never been my real friends, and I didn't really care what they thought of me. Not anymore.

And then, of course there was the whole *I'm not for sale* thing. But…I knew Phillip well enough to know he wasn't that kind of guy. So despite how it sounded, he wasn't the type of man to mean anything derogatory with his offer.

And that was the whole problem, and the only real reason I could think of not to do it.

It was *Phillip*.

Britt was right; I did have a *thing* for him. And I was pretty sure he had one for me. Always had. There were feelings there. And even if I were entertaining that possibility—and I couldn't possibly—I'd just *stolen* from him. Which made me...ugh. A terrible person.

And would I really be able to pretend there was nothing between us? That I didn't have heart palpitations every time I looked at him? Never mind how he made me feel when he *touched* me. Was I strong enough, or a good enough actress? Even for one night?

I wasn't sure.

I ignored the intense way Britt stared at me, as if she could see exactly what I was thinking and instead focused on Jessie, who sat across from me with her glass of white wine.

She spun the stem of the glass between her fingers. "But do you really have a choice?" Her voice was soft and full of concern. "You'll lose your job if you don't, right?"

I nodded and then added a shrug.

Phillip was a fair man, and I *had* stolen from him. But I didn't really think he'd take it so far that I'd lose my job. Not really. I couldn't shake the idea that there was more to this offer than that. *Much more.*

"Why would you take the money?" Britt's voice was sharp from across the table. There was nothing but water in her glass; she saved alcohol for very rare occasions, and then it was a simple vodka and soda. Although I couldn't remember the last time I'd actually seen her drink one. "You know I would have given you—"

"No." I cut her off. "I will not take money from you." I looked around the table at my friends' faces. Even though Britt was the only one with means to help me out financially, they had all offered their help when Daniel was arrested. "I could never ask that of any of you."

Britt shook her head and looked away.

"Well, I say go for it," Darla said. "I mean, what's the worst that could happen? You have a little fun? Maybe some hot sex? What could be wrong with that?"

I flushed, but didn't bother denying that the idea of hot sex, especially with Phillip, did sound appealing. *Very* appealing.

"I never did have sex with Phillip." The words slipped from my mouth before I could stop them.

"What?" I thought Jessie's eyes might fall out of her head. "I totally thought...but he...and you...I mean..." She swallowed hard and tried again. "You guys dated for..."

I shrugged. "We just never...we were waiting."

"Waiting?" Britt all but choked on her water. She stared, open-mouthed, at me. "For what exactly?"

"For—"

"Do not say marriage," Britt challenged.

I shrugged. The truth was, I didn't have an answer. Not a real one anyway.

"Really?" Sandy asked. "That's so romantic," she continued. "You were going to wait until marriage? That's what Greg and I did too. It was so special to wait for the wedding night and—"

"But Abby and Phillip *didn't* get married," Jessie interrupted. "Remember?"

Sandy, jerked out of what had obviously been a memory of her and her deceased husband, blinked hard and nodded. "Right," she said. "I know. I just..."

"It's okay." I put my hand over hers and squeezed gently, once more reminded of our differences. "With Phillip, it was just different. Like we were waiting, but I don't really know why." I shrugged and moved to the default explanation I'd settled on all those years ago, and reverted to again now. "I think he just wasn't that into me, to be honest."

"Bullshit!" Darla slapped her palm on the tabletop. "You could have been blind and still seen the way he looked at you."

"That doesn't make any—"

"I agree," Britt joined in. "He always did have a way of looking at you as if he was imagining you completely naked."

He did?

"Well, that settles it," Darla said.

I looked among my friends. "Settles what?"

"This is your chance," Darla continued. "It's exactly what you've both been waiting for. I don't know why you two didn't hook up years ago, but here you are, so go have some crazy hot sex and get it out of your system. Get *him* out of your system."

"Her system?" Sandy looked horrified. "I don't think that's how it works."

"That's exactly how it works," Britt said.

I should probably have been more disturbed at the way Darla and Britt were agreeing on this particular subject. The two of them rarely saw eye to eye about men or sex or…well, much of anything.

Sandy shook her head. "But what if it's about more than getting him out of her system?" she challenged. "Besides, it's not okay to offer her what he did."

"You mean a weekend with a super-hot man in lieu of not losing her job?" Jessie tossed back the rest of her wine and reached for the bottle. "I don't know. I think if someone made me that offer, I might just consider it."

I laughed, but Sandy was horrified. "You would not!"

"It's been a hot minute." Jessie lifted her wine glass. "Or two, or three, or…well, let's just say it's been a *long* time."

Britt laughed and raised her glass of water to clink with Jessie's.

"I think all of us could use a little bit more fun, a.k.a. *sex* in our lives!" All eyes turned to Darla, who shrugged. "I mean, except me, obviously. I already have lots of fun and a whole lot of sex. But you guys? When was the last time you had a one-night stand with a man whose name you didn't even know, Sandy?"

Sandy turned bright red and ducked her head. They all knew the answer—never. As she'd just admitted, she'd been a virgin when she'd married Greg, and since he passed away four years ago, she hadn't so much as looked at another man.

"And what about you, Jessie? Can you remember the last time you climaxed so hard you couldn't even remember your own name?"

"Darla!"

"I'll take that as a no." She laughed and turned to Britt. "I'm not even going to ask you the last time you had something between your legs that wasn't battery operated."

Brittany narrowed her eyes, but she didn't deny it was true.

"Come on, ladies. We're in our forties—we're not dead! Remember when we were young, and we promised that we wouldn't let each other get old and boring? Well…"

It was true, and exactly what I'd been thinking of for the last few weeks. We'd gotten old long before we should have. I dropped my head and stared into my glass. I'd been so busy being a socialite wife, throwing the *right* parties, going to all the *right* events, wearing the *right* thing, that it had been years since I'd done anything *right* for me at all. And Darla had a point: we weren't dead yet. Far from it. Besides…*Phillip*. Maybe Britt was right and it was time I got him out of my system once and for all.

What was the worst that could happen? Some hot, no-strings sex? I could think of a whole lot of things worse than that.

I picked up my glass and downed the rest of my martini in one gulp. "I'm going to say yes," I declared. "And hopefully I'll have a whole lot of fun while I'm at it."

Chapter Three

I KNEW she would say yes.

Abigail was too stubborn for anything else. It was one of the things I loved about her.

Loved.

I pushed the word out of my consciousness. The same way I'd been doing for years. Being so close to her, yet with so much distance between us all this time, had been my own penance for letting her go to Daniel without fighting for her. It was my loss. A terrible loss with no chance of redemption. Until now.

The day after my indecent proposal, I walked into the pro shop for her answer. She'd looked me straight in the eyes—a challenge? Maybe. And without wavering, she'd agreed.

That was two days ago, and I'd thought of little else.

I would have an entire weekend of Abigail all to myself. Well, mostly to myself. Forty-eight hours where I would have her in my home. On my arm and in my—no. I would presume nothing.

Although having her in my bed would be the ultimate goal, we were a long way from that. And despite everything, I was a gentleman. At least, I'd do my best to act like one. Besides, as much as I regretted *waiting* with Abigail all those years ago, that's not what this weekend was about. Not even close. This weekend was about so much more than simply sex.

I knew the moment she arrived. The air around me shifted. It was electric. I could *feel* it.

She was here.

A quick glance at the app on my phone that showed me my security cameras proved I was right.

She drove an old beater car that had more rust on it than paint. I cringed. Her asshole husband had screwed her over in the worst way. I hated Daniel for what he'd done to her. How he'd used her almost from the very beginning. Hell, had he ever really loved her? I couldn't allow myself to think of the alternative, that he'd been with her just to take her from me.

Dammit.

I knew it was true. And I'd let it happen. It was because of me that Abigail had ever ended up with Daniel. It was my fault that he'd destroyed her socially and financially. Not that Abigail gave any fucks about her social status. She'd always had her group of solid, real friends. The women at the country club were anything but real. Or friends.

Still, she didn't deserve the treatment she'd received from those women after her husband's scandal broke. She hadn't deserved any of it. I owed her the opportunity for a little retribution. Having her on my arm tomorrow night at the party would raise eyebrows and get tongues wagging. But more importantly, Abigail would have the opportunity to stand proud in front of those terrible women and show them that despite their best efforts, they couldn't bring her down. And that's exactly what I was hoping for. Well, that was part of what I was hoping for.

Again, my mind went right back to that dirty, sexy place. How could it not?

I watched on the screen as Abigail moved from the car and grabbed a duffel bag of her things. She wouldn't be needing any of them. I'd seen to that. My cock twitched at the thought of the gifts I'd chosen specifically for her. I knew I was walking a fine line with her. A *very* fine line. But she deserved nice things. Hell, she deserved *all* the nice things. And if I knew Abigail the way I used to, she'd love everything I'd selected.

I probably should have turned the screen off, but I couldn't seem to stop myself and I spent the next few minutes watching her through the app as she was greeted by my housekeeper, Mrs. Mclean. The older woman had been in my employ since I'd made my first millions and she had a sharp memory. She hadn't said, but I knew she remembered Abigail well enough. No doubt the older woman also knew exactly why I'd never married, or seriously dated since Abigail, too.

She was more than a house manager. She was like family to me. Mrs. Mclean knew me better than I knew myself some days. She was smart and discreet, and I knew she'd take good care of Abigail, the same way she took special care with everything in my life that was critically important to me.

I kept the volume off the screen and watched while Mrs. Mclean took Abigail's bag from her and led her up the stairs toward the room where she'd be staying. I swallowed hard against the lump that had formed in my throat. Having Abigail so close, yet still down the hall from me, was a strange, almost surreal feeling. The last time she'd been in the house, she'd turned the other way down the hall. To the primary suite. *My* suite. And that's where I wanted her again. In my room. In my bed.

That was a long time ago. A lot had changed.

I clicked off the app as they arrived at Abigail's room. I didn't have cameras in the rooms and even if I did, I wouldn't watch. Again, I was a gentleman. And having Abigail here was far more important to me than just the one weekend.

I'd be patient.

It had been years since I'd been in Phillip's home. A lifetime ago. My stomach flipped and a rush of feelings slammed into me as I followed Mrs. Mclean down the hall. Did she remember me? Certainly she must have. There'd been a time when I'd spent a lot of time here.

I even thought I might live here one day. With Phillip.

Things changed.

And here we were.

Some of the furnishings had changed, but the feel of the home was the same. The floor was laid with black and white marble. The walls were light gray and the overall feeling was one of power, masculinity, and money. Involuntarily, a shiver ran through me. Once upon a time, there'd been fresh flowers on every available surface. Purples, pinks, blues, and yellows. The blooms had lightened the stuffiness of the house. Warmed it up and made it welcoming.

I stopped before a side table that had once held a massive display of my favorites. Carnations. Such a simple flower, but gorgeous in their simplicity. Once Phillip knew I liked them, almost overnight they'd filled vases in the house. Often with other flowers to complement them. But sometimes, as it was with the large bouquet on the side table, the carnations got to be the star of the arrangement.

It was silly really, but an overwhelming pang of loss hit me in the gut as I stared at the now empty table. I felt like I might cry, and I almost never cried.

"I hope you'll find your room to your liking." Mrs. Mclean chattered on as I followed her through the long halls.

I knew I would find it very much to my liking. Mrs. Mclean was amazing at what she did. Which was everything. If she had anything to do with my room, it would be gorgeous. We walked up a long, curving staircase and took the stairs that branched off to the right, leading to yet another impossibly long hallway. She stopped in front of a set of large double doors and waited for me to catch up before she opened them with a flourish and stepped inside what was easily the most beautifully appointed room I'd ever seen.

Just as I'd expected.

It was perfect.

The entire suite was at least twice the size of the shoebox apartment I'd been renting and far bigger than the master bedroom I had in the home I'd shared with Daniel before it had been seized. But then again, Phillip had always had more money than Daniel. A fact Daniel had always resented. "He might have more money, but I got you." I shuddered at the memory of the way he'd boast about *having* me or *winning* me.

What had I ever seen in him? How could I have been so blind? To everything.

Unlike the rest of the house, the room Mrs. Mclean showed me was feminine. And very...*me*. It was painted in a soft pink color. Floor-to-ceiling windows covered one wall; gauzy curtains floated in a light breeze coming from the open window. The huge four-poster canopy king-sized bed was the feature of the space. It was made up with a pink floral duvet and more pillows than I could count. It looked like a marsh-mallow that I couldn't wait to fall into.

"It's beautiful," I breathed as I stepped into the space. My feet sank into the plush carpet.

"Mr. Conrad will be pleased you're satisfied with the accommodations."

"Satisfied?" I walked to the window, pushed the curtain aside, and gazed out over the grounds. My eyes lingered on the pool, surrounded with plants and gardens that gave it the feel of an oasis in a desert. Maybe I'd have time to sneak down for a swim? It had been a long time since I'd enjoyed that luxury.

"Mr. Conrad has selected your wardrobe for the weekend." The housekeeper's voice shattered my thoughts, reminding me exactly why I was in Phillip's house in the first place. "You will find it in the walk-in closet through the en suite bathroom."

I spun around and stared, open-mouthed, at her. "He's done what?"

She ignored me. "He's requested that you dress in something appropriate and report to his study at four o'clock sharp. You should knock twice and wait in the hallway." She moved to leave.

Was she serious?

Anger bubbled up inside me. How dare he have specific requirements for how I was to *behave?* It was outrageous.

As was the entire reason I was there in his house in the first place. But that was a detail I was choosing not to focus on for the time being. The point was, I was there. And now...

Sigh.

Now I made the best of it and got through the next few days.

The fact that I didn't want to just *get through* the next few days was very much at the forefront of my mind, but again, I pushed those thoughts from my head.

One thing at a time.

I pulled myself from my thoughts in time to see Mrs. Mclean moving toward the door.

A surge of unease and something that started to feel annoy-ingly like panic rushed through me. "Wait!"

She stopped and turned, with a small smile on her face.

Did she know what I was thinking? About why I was there? About why I was really there? Did I even know?

I wasn't used to being so unsure of myself, and it was becoming increasingly annoying.

Mrs. Mclean waited patiently for me to say something else, so I blurted out the first thing I could think of.

"Where's the study?"

Despite the fact that we both knew that I knew exactly where the study was, she gave me instructions before she slipped from the room, closing the door behind her. When she was gone, I looked to the clock on the wall. It was already quarter to four. I had only fifteen minutes to get dressed, what-ever that meant, and *report* to Phillip.

I probably should have been annoyed or even offended by his presumption that he could *dress* me and order me around, but oddly, I wasn't. In fact, I was more than a little turned on by the thought. Phillip always did have a way of taking control of a situation that was sexy. Besides, I'd made the decision to be there. I could choose what I did or did not want to do while I was there.

And I'd already decided that Darla was right. We were way too young not to have a little fun—or maybe, if I got really lucky, a lot of fun. I'd spent far too long pretending to be some-thing I wasn't. I was overdue for some excitement. And what if the forties really were the new twenties? Only better?

There was only one way to find out.

I shot the girls a quick text to let them know that I'd arrived safely. I took a quick photo of the decadently plush bed and hit Send before powering off my phone. No doubt the picture would spark all types of comments. Most of them inappropriate. I was curious for sure, but I was running out of time if I didn't want to keep Phillip waiting. And to my surprise, I found that I didn't. Not even a little bit.

With a devilish grin on my face, I went to explore the rest of my accommodations but almost didn't get past the bathroom. Setting foot in the white marble room was just like a visit to the spa. From what I remembered. One breath of the peppermint and lavender scent that filled the air, and I was drawn like a magnet to the oversized bathtub set in the corner. What I wouldn't give to sink into a tub full of hot, steamy bubbles.

How long had it been since I'd immersed myself in the simple joy of a bath?

Too long.

I closed my eyes and inhaled, letting the smell fill my senses before I opened my eyes again. When I did, my gaze landed on two huge double doors on the opposite side of the massive bathroom.

The closet.

I couldn't help but feel a little overdramatic as I pulled the closet doors open with a flourish. But the drama faded into pure astonishment as the closet and its contents were revealed.

My mouth fell open.

There was room enough for an entire store's worth of clothing in the space that was easily double the size of the bedroom in my apartment. Most of the room was empty, with only one rack on the far side that held clothes. I crossed the space to see what my choices were.

It was an interesting mix of garments and despite the fact that I'd only agreed to stay for the weekend, there were enough outfits for at least a month.

Phillip had beautiful taste, I'd give him that. And each item had obviously been chosen specifically with me in mind.

There was a floor-length gown in a royal blue that I knew would make my eyes pop, but it wasn't the color the caught my attention. It was quite possibly the sexiest and most gorgeous dress I'd ever seen. No doubt he wanted me to wear that to the club the next night. The other women's mouths would fall open and their husband's eyes would all be on me. I grinned in anticipation, because there was no doubt Phillip also knew exactly what would happen. I secretly loved how his mind worked.

I quickly examined the other few articles hanging up, all beautiful dresses. None quite as elegant as the blue gown, but all equally stunning and *very* expensive. No doubt each dress cost more than I made in a month at the club.

I turned my attention to the dresser.

The moment I slid the first large drawer out, heat flooded to my face. *Phillip had chosen this?*

I'd never seen lingerie that was both gorgeous and so completely slutty all at the same time. I pulled out a pale-pink silk corset. There were matching thong panties with an accompanying garter in the same soft pink.

What. The. Hell?

It was one thing for him to pick out a few dresses for me to wear, but lingerie? My face flushed. There was no way he remembered how much I used to enjoy wearing things like this. *Was there?* Those days felt like a million years ago. It had all been different with Daniel.

But Phillip had remembered.

We were still so young when we'd dated, but I'd recently discovered how good sexy lingerie felt. I'd reveled in the silk and lace. But mostly, I'd loved the fact that when I was wearing it, no one else knew what was under my clothes.

No one except Phillip. Even though we'd never taken our relationship all to the next level, we'd come pretty damn close, and it had been hot. I'd loved to tease him with little peeks of what was under my dress when we went out to dinner. Seeing his excitement only increased my own enjoyment.

But that was a long time ago.

I dropped the corset on the pile of silky things.

I hadn't worn anything like that in far too long. Daniel was never a lingerie guy. He used to say that he never saw the point of spending so much money on something you just took off right away.

But Phillip...he obviously understood.

And I couldn't figure out how that made me feel. A kaleidoscope of feelings rushed through me. Guilt for taking the money in the first place—I wasn't Daniel. I never should have done that. But it couldn't have been all bad. After all, it had brought me here. To Phillip. And I would be lying if I said there wasn't more than curiosity there when it came to him. There was much more. There always had been.

I lifted the lingerie again.

What was he thinking with this?

Did he expect me to wear these things? For him?

The idea of wearing any of these items for Phillip sent a thrill through me.

But would I?

Was he feeling the same way I was? Confused? Turned on? Guilty?

"Go have some crazy hot sex and get it out of your system." Darla's voice echoed in my brain.

Yes. I would wear them.

But did he *expect* me to? Or did he *want* me to? There was a difference. And I needed to know which it was.

With the pink corset still clutched in my hands, I left my bedroom suite, went down the curved staircase, and marched through the grand hallways. My confusion grew with each step until I found the door to his study. I didn't bother knocking. I turned the handle and shoved the door open. It slammed roughly against the wall, and Phillip Conrad looked up from his desk as if he'd been expecting me.

He probably was.

"Abigail." The flicker of humor in his voice only made me more upset. "You aren't dressed. Didn't you like what I picked out?" He chuckled and leaned back in his chair.

So cocky.

"Did I get the size wrong?"

He scanned me up and down, a move that from anyone else I'd find offensive. Hell, I should have found it offensive coming from him.

But I didn't.

I momentarily forgot why I'd gone in search of him in the first place. I was completely transfixed by him and the mixture of feelings he elicited in me. The power and wealth and control he exuded simply from sitting in his chair behind his massive oak desk radiated from him in waves. Never mind the way he was looking at me. I could see it in his eyes. Maybe after all this time, he needed to get me out of his system, too. And he thought by buying me lingerie, that would be a given.

Damn. That was beyond cocky.

"You aren't dressed," he said again when I still hadn't spoken.

His words snapped me back to why I was there. I shook the corset in my hand. "Did you really think that by buying me some cheap shit like this, I'd just jump into bed with you?" I couldn't even believe the words coming out of my mouth. Did I even care if that's what had happened? Wasn't that why I was there, too?

Yes.

No.

Shit. I didn't know.

I stepped forward and tossed the corset on the desk in front of him.

Phillip looked down at the item in front of him and then slowly got to his feet. "Cheap?" He picked up the corset. "You think this hand-stitched, custom-made silk work of art is cheap?" He glanced down at the garment and then his eyes landed on me, pinning me in place.

"It's not the quality," I argued. "It's that I'll look...I can't dress like a..."

"Like a what?" he challenged.

"Like a whore!" I spat out the word and instantly regretted it. That's not at all what I thought about Phillip. He would never...Phillip wasn't that kind of guy. My thoughts crashed through me, and I couldn't make sense of anything. Being so near to him was messing with my mind. My heart clenched as I watched his handsome face twist into a mask of horror. I'd made a horrible mistake.

"Oh God, Abigail. No! I would never—"

"Then why? I mean, I took the money and I'm sorry, but I don't think—" *Shit.* I'd just confessed, and I could see that he'd noticed, too.

To his credit, he didn't mention it. "I would never insinuate anything of that sort, Abigail, and I think you know that."

I did.

But so many feelings were crashing through me. It was as if I were having an out-of-body experience. The combination of my guilt for taking the money, his offer, the fact that I'd accepted because I wanted to be close to him, and the feelings I couldn't even begin to make sense of, combined with being there, in his house and seeing the lingerie...years of questions and no answers, feelings that had never gone away—it was all too much.

I gulped for a breath. I needed something, anything, to center me. But what I really should do was get the hell out of there. I should just turn around and walk away before I made a bigger fool of myself, before I said something I really couldn't take back. But I couldn't move. I was completely transfixed by him.

Phillip had moved around the table. He looked as if he wanted to touch me, maybe try to convince me that no, that's not what he was inferring. And truthfully, I didn't really think he was. Phillip just wasn't like that. I knew that deep in my soul. Despite what I'd accused him of.

I tried not to tremble as he stood only inches from me.

"You don't really think that of me, do you?"

I swallowed hard and opened my mouth to object, but he held up a finger and pressed it to my lips.

"I have nothing but respect for you." His voice was smooth and slow. "You can leave anytime you want. And I won't report you to management. I'll even let you keep the money. That's not what this was about. That's not what this was ever about."

Was he really saying what I thought he was? He was letting me off the hook?

Of course he was. It was never about the money. We both knew it.

But...no! I didn't want to leave. I definitely didn't want to be let *off the hook.*

The thought crashed into me hard and a hot pool of need settled between my legs as I realized I was exactly where I wanted to be. Here. With him.

I inhaled slowly, and making my decision, snatched the corset from his hand, spun on my heel, and left him standing behind me.

Chapter Four

SHE LEFT.

Or did she?

The space she'd occupied only a moment before felt empty. She'd been so close. I could smell her shampoo. Peaches and honey. That hadn't changed.

I lifted my hand into the empty space and dropped it to my side.

Shit.

I wasn't used to being out of control. Ever. I'd made an entire career of being in control of every moment, in every single situation. I knew how people were going to react before they did. I anticipated every move. In every way.

Except with Abigail. I'd never been able to predict how she'd behave.

Clearly that hadn't changed over the years, because I didn't really think she'd leave. I thought she'd appreciate the gesture. I thought maybe she would have seen past the pretense for getting her here. I thought...hell, I didn't know what I thought.

But I sure *hoped* she felt the same way about me that I did about her. That maybe after all these years, she might still have some sort of feelings for me. That maybe it was *finally* our time to figure out where we'd gone wrong all those years ago. But maybe I'd blown it again. Maybe I'd pushed too hard. I'd chosen the dresses for her because they were sexy and classy at the same time, yet they pushed the limits of what that stuffy, pretentious small-town country club could handle. And I knew Abigail would love to push every single one of those limits.

The lingerie…that might have been a step too far. But despite her reaction, I didn't think so. I *knew* Abigail. Correction. I had *known* her. But the Abigail I'd known had loved her lingerie.

She'd lost so much. Everything in her life was ripped from her through no fault of her own, and it seemed like such a small thing to offer her a little bit of extravagance. Lingerie had been her secret splurge all those years ago, and even though I'd never personally unwrapped her from any of those sexy, lacy treats she used to wear while we dated, I remembered them well. I also remembered exactly how they'd made my body come alive with just one glance.

Damn.

Why had I never taken our relationship to the next level? It was a question I'd tortured myself with for over fifteen years. But as much as I'd wanted to, I'd known then that Abigail was special. Too special to rush in to things with. I was going to ask her to marry me first. Make sure she knew exactly how I felt about her. But then Daniel had come home from Europe.

And Daniel always got everything he'd wanted.

I'd been a fool to let him have Abigail, too. And without a fight. I'd just stepped away like the weak coward I'd been.

But I'd changed.

I'd spent the last fifteen years becoming a man strong enough, powerful enough, and confident enough to be worthy of her.

And now, I'd blown it…again.

Fuck.

I turned and slammed my fist down on the desk, hard. Before I could do it again, I heard the creak of the door behind me.

"So? What do you think?"

My whole body stiffened at the sound of her voice deepened with desire. I knew before turning what I would see.

But knowing what you'd see and actually *seeing* it were two very different things. Especially when it came to a woman like Abigail. Which was why, when I turned around, I sucked in a sharp breath at the exquisite sight of my first and only real love, looking every bit the goddess she most certainly was.

The corset I'd chosen for her—because I knew she'd secretly love the sweet, feminine color—looked far more sinful than sweet on her body. The boning of the garment narrowed her already slim waist further, creating curves that my hands itched to touch. Her breasts were pushed so far up, they almost spilled right out the top. She wore the matching panties, which I knew were only a scrap of lace. And sure enough, when she turned in a slow spin to show me the entire effect, and her perfectly round peach bottom was fully exposed to me, it was confirmed.

Unwittingly, I let out a low growl and stepped toward her. "What are you doing, Abigail?"

She turned to me, her face a mixture of defiance and desire. "Isn't this why you bought it? Because you wanted to see it?"

Ohh, she was playing a game, that much was certain. But it was a dangerous game. In more ways than one. And she had no idea.

Or maybe she did.

My arousal had to be more than evident if she dared look.

And she did.

Damn.

I didn't miss the way her nostrils flared, her eyes narrowed in challenge as she refocused on me.

"Abigail." I worked hard to keep my voice under control. As it was, it came out lower and gruffer than I wanted it to. But I couldn't help it. The sight of her was doing things to me that were making it very hard to focus. Still. I needed to stay in control. "You don't want to—"

"You have no idea what I want."

Oh, I was pretty sure I did. I just didn't know *why.*

Her tongue slipped from between her lips and licked slowly along her plump bottom lip.

Two steps and I was in front of her. Without thinking, I grabbed her forearms and held her tight. The need to kiss her, to taste her after all this time, was almost too strong to resist.

Almost.

She tipped her head up, her eyes closed.

More than anything I wanted to feel her lips on mine, her body pressed against mine.

I inhaled slowly. She waited.

No. Not like this.

I released her and swiftly walked back to my desk, where I put both hands flat against the hard surface and dropped my head, dragging in one deep breath after another.

I couldn't breathe with her so close. Let alone half naked.

Behind me, I heard her make a noise. But before I could react, Abigail grabbed my arm and tugged. I spun around to see her beautiful face flushed a sexy shade of red, her mouth set in a line of determination.

"Abigail, I—"

"I told you," she interrupted me. "My name is Abby."

She pushed her slight body up against me. Hard. She moved a bare leg between mine and pressed her thigh against my throbbing erection, right before she took my face in two hands and kissed me.

I hoped like hell I wasn't making a mistake. It was a risk, to be sure. But…

There was something between us. There always had been. It would just be better to get it out of the way. The tension, the unspoken need.

No more games.

And besides, Darla had a point. It was long past time for me to get Phillip Conrad out of my system. And what could be a more perfect time? Maybe it would give me clarity. Maybe I'd finally know once and for all if what I thought I was feeling was real. Besides, he had bought me the lingerie. He couldn't even pretend it wasn't what he wanted, too.

But damn him, he was clearly going to make me work for it.

Fine.

If that's what it took…

I wasn't the same unsure, scared twenty-something he remembered. That Abby had stood by and let the man she loved cast her aside. Phillip had all but handed her to Daniel, as if what they'd shared hadn't been real. And it had. She'd felt it with every cell in her body. But still, she'd let it happen.

That Abby hadn't been confident enough to challenge Phillip, to ask him why. Instead, she'd been hurt. *So hurt.*

If I'd only been stronger back then, maybe I could have fought for what I was so sure we shared instead of letting it slip away.

But I'd changed. I'd learned. And I knew enough now that if I was ever going to get what I wanted, I had to go after it.

So I kissed him.

And the moment my lips touched his, all of my bravado melted away because...*damn.*

I definitely wasn't going to be able to get him *out of my system.* The touch of his lips had stirred up a whole lot more than unfinished business.

Taken off guard, Phillip's lips resisted, but only for a second before they softened and melted into the kiss. For a second, I feared he might push me away again, but then one hand clamped around my waist to hold me tight, while the other twined through my hair as his tongue found mine and plunged into my mouth, deepening the kiss.

Yes. This was what I'd wanted. And so much more. Phillip had always kissed me as if his life depended on it. As if he needed me to breathe. That hadn't changed.

My entire body lit up with a desire so intense my knees buckled. I groaned and pressed into him harder, using my thigh to rub his swollen erection.

He moaned and used my hair to tug my head back before his mouth found the sensitive skin on my neck. He sucked, nipped, and even bit down a little; the slight shot of pain traveled through me and intensified the throbbing between my legs.

It had been far too long since I'd been kissed this way. As if every beat of my heart were dependent on Phillip's mouth on mine. His lips gave me life. Fueled me in a way I'd forgotten I needed simply to exist. After so many years, I once again came alive under his attentions and could no longer remember how I'd survived so long without him.

When I'd slipped the corset on over my curves, it was in challenge. I wanted to push him, test him. Maybe even piss him off a little bit. Sure, I'd wanted this. Probably more than I cared to admit to myself, but now…

There were so many feelings, *too* many, jumbling my thoughts. But when his lips traveled up my throat and found my mouth once more, everything became clear again. I wanted more. I *needed* more.

As if answering my unasked plea, he slid his hands down my body and over my exposed bottom. He cupped my flesh and squeezed, before scooping me up. A moan escaped from somewhere deep down as I wrapped my legs around his waist and pressed against him, kissing him with abandon.

Phillip turned me around and set me on the cool, smooth wood of his desk.

Yes.

Finally.

I groaned and tipped my head back as his hands worked their way down my body, exploring and teasing over the pink silk and lace of the corset until his fingers slipped beneath the elastic of the scrap of panties and found how wet and ready for him I was.

It was bold. Maybe it was *too* bold. Six months ago, I would never have done this. But maybe that was the point. I'd spent way too much time playing it safe, not letting myself feel what I deserved to feel. Not allowing my desires to take center stage.

No more.

"Yes." The word was a moan on my lips as he slid one finger and then another into my heat. "Phillip." I rocked against his hand. "It's always been…" My words faded away and he stilled. Waiting. "I…"

I couldn't do it. I couldn't bring myself to tell him how I felt.

How could I when I couldn't even admit it to myself?

Taking the safer route, I chickened out and simply said, "I missed you."

His pupils dilated and it was enough for him to continue his attentions on me. But I needed more, and I wasn't going to be able to wait for it. I'd waited long enough. While he moved inside me, I reached for the zipper on his pants and drew it down.

Phillip sucked in a breath and froze. "Abigail, I—"

"No." I cut him off before he could slow it down. I didn't want slow. I slipped my hand past the fabric of his boxer briefs and wrapped it around the hard length of him. He groaned. "After all," I said slowly before licking my bottom lip. "We should have done this years ago. It's long past time, don't you think?" It was *certainly* what I thought. But he was the reason we were here. "This was your plan all—"

He jerked away from me so quickly I almost lost my balance on the desk. I felt the loss of his nearness, of his fingers, of his touch, as if he'd thrown a bucket of water on me.

"What the…"

Phillip had turned away from me and was zipping his pants before I even realized what had happened.

My mind raced. *What the hell?* He'd set this up. He'd planned it all. He'd bought the sexy lingerie. I was so confused. He *had* to want this the way I did.

And I *did*. I wanted *him*.

"You should go."

"Phillip, I…" I what? "I'm sorry…" I wasn't exactly sure what I was apologizing for. The money? For coming on to him? For saying whatever it was that I said that stopped this? For not being able to be honest with my feelings?

I didn't know. And it didn't matter because he still wouldn't look at me.

He was rejecting me, *again.*

No. I shook my head. *Not again.*

"No." Confusion, hurt, and rejection welled up in me. Still, he didn't turn around. "I mean, yes. I am sorry. But I…I just don't know why I'm here, Phillip, and I…" I blinked hard. I would not cry. Not now that I'd just thrown myself at him and he'd pushed me away.

There was only so much one woman could take.

"Do you know why I'm here?" I lowered my voice, unsure I could say what I was thinking. It was easier that he wasn't looking at me. I took a deep breath. "Not because you made me a deal, or I did something I shouldn't have, or because I was scared to lose my job." I swallowed hard.

"I'm here because it was *you,* Phillip. Because it's always been…"

I couldn't even believe what I was saying. All these years and I'd never even allowed myself to *think* such things, let alone say them aloud.

And I couldn't make sense of what was happening. The way he kissed me. He felt it, too. I knew he did. I just didn't understand what was happening now.

Hot tears threatened, and I swallowed back a sob. I would *not* cry in front of him.

When he turned to look at me, I saw the pain and hurt in his eyes for the first time. The confusion and the…what?

"It's always been what?" He didn't wait for an answer. He scrubbed a hand over his face and shook his head. "I don't blame you if you want to leave. And as I said before, the deal is off. You can go whenever you want. I don't want you to ever… I can't bear you thinking anything less of me. I didn't mean for it to turn out that way," he continued, leaving me with more questions than answers. "That's not what this is about, Abigail. Not for me."

He turned again and walked to the window, his back to me.

The breath had been sucked from my lungs. I was deflated. Empty. I'd taken a risk. A *big* one. I'd been bold. Gone after what I wanted. What I thought we *both* wanted. And...

I'd been dismissed. Or discarded.

Confused and more hurt than I cared to admit, I did the only thing I could think of to do.

I left.

Chapter Five

I DIDN'T DESERVE HER.

I didn't deserve her then. And I didn't now.

The moment the door shut behind her, I sagged against my desk, letting my head fall heavy between my arms.

It had taken every ounce of self-control I possessed to walk away from Abigail just then. Having her in my arms again after so many years apart had been more intoxicating than I could have predicted. Every part of her: her scent, her touch, the feel of her skin, the sight of her luscious curves encased in silk and lace, the sound of her moans...

She'd put every single one of my senses on high alert and my body had reacted intensely. I wanted her. Badly.

But it was about more than her body. More than sex.

It always had been.

And that's why I'd waited.

I forced myself to stand up and take a deep breath. I moved to the window and looked out over the sprawling gardens outside. The sun was setting and the lights that had been placed throughout the flower beds and twisting paths started to illuminate the dusky shadows.

Day or night, the gardens calmed me. They always did. I didn't move until my breathing was once more regular and even.

I wasn't going to be any good—especially to Abigail—if I couldn't keep my composure. And she deserved me at my best. The way I should have behaved years ago. Instead, I'd failed her. And myself.

Five years her senior, and being raised in completely different social circles, we'd never crossed paths before the day I'd quite literally run into her at the grocery store. She was buying a basket full of fresh vegetables to make a salad for her dinner. My own basket was full of microwavable meals and snacks. Mrs. Mclean was off for the weekend and although I'd turned out to be a whiz at security systems and turning them into a multimillion-dollar business almost overnight, I'd yet to master making myself a simple dinner.

She'd laughed at me and offered to share her salad with me. I would have been a fool to turn down that radiant smile and twinkling brown eyes full of mischief. And I didn't.

We were inseparable after that. We'd only been together for about four months, but they'd been some of the best of my life. Every day I spent with Abigail was a good one. Our days were spent laughing and kissing. Our nights were spent doing even more kissing, and a little bit more, always stopping short before taking it to the next level. I'd been a gentleman. Not wanting to rush her. Or our relationship. We had time, after all.

I was so sure we had the rest of our lives together.

Turned out I was wrong.

The memory of that night hadn't faded even a little bit over the years. Every detail was just as vivid as when it happened. I squeezed my eyes shut and there she was, young Abigail. She wore a simple white sundress; her dark hair fell in soft waves over her bare shoulders. Her cheeks were pinked from the sun and from laughing.

Everything was perfect. A few months earlier, I'd moved into my house. The gardens had sold me on the property that was far too large and ostentatious for me. But the gardens... Besides, if everything went according to plan, it wouldn't be only me in the house for very long.

I'd laid out a picnic on the lawn, surrounded by the lilac bushes that were in full bloom. I'd just poured the wine and handed Abigail a glass. She looked so sweet, and almost innocent in her sundress. Although I knew the truth, and my love was far from innocent. The night before had been a testament to exactly how naughty she could be. It had taken more self-control than I even knew I possessed to hold myself back from consummating our relationship right then and there.

And maybe I should have. Holding her at bay had hurt her feelings. I'd seen it in her face. She was confused by the way I wanted to wait before having sex. Hell, I was confused too. But then again, I'd never felt this way about a woman before and I didn't want to screw it up.

Besides, that was the night I planned to finally tell her—and show her—exactly how I felt. The night I planned to finally tell Abigail that I was head over heels in love with her.

And ask her to marry me.

It was a big leap. A definite risk, especially because I'd still not told her that I loved her. And it wasn't because I wasn't sure. I was. Almost from that first shared salad, I knew. She was the one for me.

And I was pretty sure she felt the same way. *Pretty sure.*

I wasn't naturally a risk taker. Not in things that really mattered, like business and love. I evaluated the risk and made calculated decisions accordingly. Asking Abigail to marry me would be a risk. But I was willing to take it.

Still standing at my office window, I opened my eyes and gazed out toward the clearing where I'd taken her that evening. Where it all had gone wrong.

"Abigail?" She'd just taken a bite of a cracker and she smiled as she took a sip of wine before taking the hand I'd offered her. "These last few months with you have been... well..." I shook my head and laughed at myself. I was usually so confident and smooth. Nothing rattled me. Love did crazy things to a man.

I swallowed and tried again. I stroked the back of her hand with my thumb as I looked into her brown eyes. "Every moment I spend with you is so much fun and we laugh, and... well, I've never laughed like I have with you."

Her smile dipped and I rushed on, cognizant that I was screwing it up. "But it's more than just fun," I said clumsily. I was making a mess of it all, but I couldn't seem to save it so I pushed on. "I know you've been wanting to take things to the next—"

"Phillip." She cut me off and pulled her hand away from mine.

I felt the loss immediately.

"I wasn't trying to come on so strong. I was just—"

"No!" I could not let this get any more screwed up. I reached for her hand back and squeezed. "I liked it. I just..."

"Look, Phillip." She looked down at the blanket and started picking at a string. "I get it. I just—"

"No." I shook her hand in mine to make her look up. "Abigail, it's not that. I wanted to take things slow because..." I took a breath and went for it.

"I love you."

"Hey! There you are!" A deep voice called out from behind me, drowning out my words. A split second later, I felt a slap on my back and was hauled to my feet—away from Abigail—and pulled into a tight bear hug. "Thought you might be waiting to pick me up at the airport, Phil!"

Daniel.

We'd been friends since we were only three years old. Although some days—most days, lately—the term *friends* was generous.

Daniel had been in Europe for the last six months, no doubt sleeping his way through the clubs of every city he visited while he was *finding himself* or whatever it was he told his parents to convince them it was a good idea to take a leave from the family investment firm and party for the last few months.

"I didn't know you were coming back today, Daniel. I—"

"And *who* is this?"

He pushed me aside and moved straight for Abigail. Looking back, I can see how it happened in slow motion. Daniel always was charming. He always got the girl. Or *girls.* I couldn't count how many of our friends' girlfriends he'd taken just because he could.

"You are gorgeous." Daniel knelt on one knee and took Abigail's hand in his. As he brought it to his mouth and pressed his lips to her skin, I saw it happen. The flush that crept over her cheeks.

Just like that, in one moment, it all changed. It was like I was outside of myself as Abigail giggled and Daniel turned on the charm. It was supposed to have been an evening to remember. Instead, I would remember it for all the wrong reasons.

Especially because I'd told Abigail how I'd felt about her and not only had our moment been interrupted, but even worse—she'd never said it back.

And judging by the way she laughed and blushed at Daniel's advances, I'd backed off. I never could compete with him. And I hadn't been about to start then.

Biggest mistake of my life.

I'd spent over fifteen years regretting that day. I was a different man now. I wasn't about to give up on her, or what I knew we could have together so easily.

Not again.

Chapter Six

SURE. I could have walked away. And maybe I should have left. But I didn't.

After I ran out of Phillip's office, humiliated and confused, hurt and pissed off and…all the things…and I got back to my room, I hate to admit it, but I saw the shower had at least two giant shower heads in it, and a steam function, and I just couldn't pass it up.

Just one shower, I told myself. Then I'd leave.

But after spending almost an hour under the hot water, I was feeling better. Well, not better *better*, but not quite so hurt. And when I came out of the bathroom, wrapped in only a towel, I could see Mrs. Mclean had been there.

A tray with meats and cheeses, fresh fruit, and a bottle of wine was laid out on the table by the window.

I looked for a note but there wasn't one. I couldn't help but be disappointed. What? Did I expect that Phillip would send me a note? An apology? A love letter?

It was stupid and childish. But still, I couldn't help but wish he had.

I changed out the towel for a fluffy robe and flopped into

the oversized chair next to the refreshments. I popped a grape in my mouth and picked up my phone to check the group chat I had with the girls.

There were at least ten messages, all of which were some form of inquiry or speculation into what I was up to.

My friends all had very active imaginations, and I couldn't help but admire their creativity about what I could have been doing. Hell, what I *wished* I was doing. Not that I hadn't enjoyed my decadent shower experience. But still, some hot sex would have been far more preferable. Especially if it came without the humiliation of being rejected. Again.

Maybe I'd been naive to think that things had changed over the years and that he might actually want me this time around.

I poured myself a glass of wine, took a deep drink, and filled the girls in on what had actually gone down. There was no point in sparing any of the humiliating details. After all, if you couldn't be honest with your best friends, who could you be honest with?

I'd no sooner hit Send on my message when my screen lit up with an incoming group video call.

Despite the fact that the last thing I wanted to do was actually see anyone, preferring to drown my embarrassment in the delicious bottle of wine in front of me, I clicked the button that connected me first to Jessie, followed quickly by Sandy and Britt. A "DD" stood in place of Darla's face.

"Sorry, ladies." Darla's voice floated from the circle that should have been her video. "I'm not really…well, let's just say I'm not decent. And also not alone," she added quickly.

I shook my head with a chuckle. What did it matter if some random guy who was no doubt twisted around my friend's naked body at the moment listened in? It's not as if we'd ever meet him. Hell, Darla probably wouldn't even see him again.

"I thought this deserved more than just a group text," Jessie said, pressing forward with the matter at hand. "What the hell happened, Abby?"

"I thought you were there to be a date at the party tomorrow?" Jessie asked. Confusion lined her face. "Why would he buy you lingerie?" She looked at me with narrowed eyes. "And why would you model it for him?"

Darla snort-laughed. "A man only buys lingerie like that if he wants one thing."

With other men, I might have agreed, but Phillip…it wasn't like that. Not really. But how could I explain it?

"Well, obviously not," Jessie chimed in. "Not if he turned her down." She shook her head. "Why would he turn you down?"

"Clearly he's gay. Or insane." Britt was matter-of-fact.

"He's not either." I took a sip of wine. It really was good. Way better than the cheap shit I'd been drinking because it was all I could afford. "He's just…" Truthfully, I didn't know what was going on with Phillip. There'd been so many mixed signals. There was no way I'd gotten them all wrong.

I'd seen the way he looked at me. The energy between us. Everything that hadn't been said. That wasn't imagined. No way. It was very, very real. I just knew it.

But I couldn't explain it.

Instead, I took another sip of my drink.

"Well, there's a reason you're still there," Jessie said. "I think I would have left if I'd been turned down like that. My self-esteem couldn't handle it. I think it took a hit out of sympathy for _you_."

I offered her a small, supportive smile. My friend had struggled with her body image her whole life. Getting pregnant with twins and the toll it had taken on her body had only exacerbated the situation. As had her husband having an affair with another woman.

"And he did say the deal was off, right?"

I nodded at Darla's question.

"So if he's letting you off the hook *and* he wasn't in it for sex—which I still don't understand—why did you stay?"

"Right," Britt said. "Why *are* you still there?" Even through the screen, her gaze pierced me.

I swallowed hard and pulled my robe a little tighter around me. "The shower was amazing." I couldn't look at any of them as I spoke; they'd see right through me. "And the snacks... never mind the bed." I gestured to the sumptuous bed behind me. It would be like sleeping in a cloud.

"Bullshit."

My head snapped up, my eyes opened wide in shock at Sandy's choice of language. And I wasn't the only one. Even Darla had turned on her camera. Her face bore the same shocked expression as the rest of us.

"What?" Sandy pressed her lips together. "I curse sometimes."

"Um...no you don't," Jessie said.

Britt laughed, but Sandy ignored them and spoke to me. "You like him," she said. "That's why you're still there. This is about more than the money or getting him out of your system."

"There's a lot of things—"

"But I'm not wrong."

I shook my head. "No," I answered truthfully. "You're not wrong. I like him."

It was more than that, and we all knew it. But I didn't know how to properly express exactly what I was feeling, especially because I wasn't even sure of those feelings myself. But what I did know was that being with Phillip again, being in his home, in his presence…it was all sensation overload. But it had been nothing compared to how I'd felt the moment my lips touched his. Every single feeling I'd ever had that I'd thought I'd buried deep all those years ago rushed back, full force.

I hadn't left because I owed it to myself to explore those feelings after all this time. And no matter how the night had turned out, I knew there was still something between us. I'd felt it in his kiss.

And that's what I couldn't explain to my friends. Because there was no way to properly put into words how Phillip had made me feel when he put his hands on my body, his lips on mine. How I'd come alive with his touch.

The whole weekend had started with *having a little fun.* But in only a few hours, it had gone way beyond that. Now, I needed to know whether what I was feeling was real. Whether it could be more, and most importantly, whether he felt the same way after all this time.

Maybe I was overthinking all of it. But maybe I wasn't.

But there was only one way to find out.

I needed to stay.

Chapter Seven

THE BED WAS every bit as comfortable as I imagined it would be. So much so that I slept deeper than I had in months. Years, maybe. It was almost noon before I finally pulled myself from the fluffy depths of the cloud bed.

My dreams had been filled of Phillip. Not that I was surprised, given the situation. But, I was surprised by the types of dreams I'd had. Given the way we'd left things last night, I would have expected my dreams to be very X-rated, or at least have a little bit of kissing and touching.

Instead, they were exactly the opposite. Although the exact content of the dreams were just out of my reach, what I could remember was the general feeling.

It reminded me of the Disney movies I would occasionally watch with Sandy and her girls when they were younger. In the dream, I'd been surrounded by bright colors and happy music. Phillip was there, and he was smiling and holding my hand. But more than anything else, the dreams had made me feel safe. And loved.

I woke up feeling content and despite everything...happy.

Maybe it was the dream, or just blind hope, but I'd been

hoping that there would be some sort of message from Phillip. A note, or a text, or some kind of indication of what I should do, whether I was still welcome in his home, and as his date later that night. But there was nothing. I tried not to be disappointed that he didn't reach out. I didn't want to let it affect my light mood. Besides, I wasn't the type of woman to sit around and wait for things to happen. If I wanted to know what was going on, there was only one way to find out.

I wrapped the big fluffy robe around me and went in search of answers.

I found them with Mrs. Mclean in the kitchen.

"I hope you're hungry," she said, without turning around from the stove, the moment I walked in. The woman always did seem to have a sixth sense about everything that went on in the house. Phillip had hired her shortly before we'd met. I remember teasing him about needing a "woman" to hold his life together, but he wasn't embarrassed. And he never for one moment let me believe that it was a *woman* he needed to run his life.

"I want a woman to be *part* of my life. Not *organize* it." He held my face softly between his hands and stared into my eyes. "There's a huge difference," he'd said seriously. "I'm not that kind of man, Abigail. I hope you realize that's not what I'm looking for in a woman."

I nodded and swallowed the lump that had formed in my throat.

It had been the first indication that maybe Phillip felt the same way I was starting to feel. That even though we were young and hadn't been together very long, maybe what we had together was special. Maybe it could be something more?

I shook my head from the memory. I hadn't thought of that moment in years. After all, what was the point? As it had turned out, Phillip hadn't felt that way at all. The moment

Daniel showed up, he'd lost interest in me. I'd run through all the scenarios in my head: he was embarrassed to be with me, he'd grown bored, it hadn't been serious to him, he wasn't attracted to me.

Yes, I'd gone through them all many years ago. I wasn't about to do it again. It didn't matter.

I focused instead on Mrs. Mclean, who was waiting for an answer.

"Yes, thank you," I said, a little unsure about what I was agreeing to.

"Mr. Conrad left me instructions to make you eggs Benedict with a side of pink grapefruit segments." Her smile was kind. "Is that still your favorite?"

I nodded numbly. He'd remembered. Or she had. Or both.

"If you'd prefer something else, I'd be happy to—"

"No." I cut her off. "It sounds delicious." As if to confirm my words, my stomach growled in agreement. It had been a long time since the snack the night before.

"Where is, Phil—Mr. Conrad?" What *was* I supposed to call him? "Where is Phillip?" I tried again. "Is he around?" I glanced around the gleaming white kitchen as if he would appear out of nowhere. I tried not to show I was anxious, although why I was trying to hide anything from Mrs. Mclean was a mystery to me.

"Mr. Conrad is out for the day. He had something to take care of at the office."

I picked up the mug of coffee that had been poured for me. One cream, one sugar. Just the way I liked it.

"He requested that you make yourself at home and enjoy the pool if it suited you."

I hoped my disappointment didn't show on my face as I lifted the mug and inhaled the rich aroma.

"He also asked me to tell you that he would still very much

like you to accompany him tonight," Mrs. Mclean added casually.

I might have even been convinced it was just a casual afterthought, too, if it wasn't for the way she watched me closely for my reaction.

"I will."

She smiled warmly, but didn't say anything as she placed the breakfast plate in front of me. "The car will be arriving to take you both to the party at five o'clock exactly. I can send for someone to do your hair and makeup if you'd like?"

That was too much. I shook my head. "I'm fine. Thank you." I picked up the plate. "I'm going to eat on the patio, if that's okay?"

"Make yourself at home. And if there's anything at all that you need—"

"Thank you, Mrs. Mclean." My smile was genuine. I always had felt like the older woman liked me. "I'll be ready on time tonight, not to worry."

I added the last part more for Phillip than for the house-keeper, who had no real reason to worry. But if I knew Phillip, he had security cameras all over this house. After all, it was how he'd made his millions. And I also knew he'd be watching. I said I'd be there, and I would.

I wanted him to know that.

She'd stayed.

I really wasn't sure that she would. Not this time.

After she'd left my office, I'd forced myself to turn off all the cameras or anything that might alert me if she'd left. It was torture to wait and wonder all night. But I deserved it.

I didn't sleep for more than a few minutes at a time before

my subconscious would wake me up, berating me for my bull-shit behavior again and again.

What had I been thinking?

I hadn't.

And that was the problem. I'd lost control, because how could I not?

Abigail was gorgeous and sexy and smart and strong, and she'd been standing in front of me with nothing but a scrap of silk and lace on. I was a man, for fuck's sake. Not a robot! Of course I would react to that. And that kiss.

Dammit.

That woman could kiss. Always could. The connection between us always had been fire and it still was. No woman before or since could ever even remotely compare to Abigail.

Not. Even. Close.

Which was why I needed distance. Because if I didn't have it, both the night before when I pulled away and then again when the sun finally came up, I would rush things and risk ruining everything. And after all these years, that was the very last thing I wanted to do.

She wasn't ready. Not yet. Sure, she was *ready*. I groaned. She was more than ready physically, but not mentally. Not for me. Not for what I wanted from her.

That much was clear by her comments.

It fucking killed me that she would think for a second that the reason I had her in my home, in my arms, was because I thought she was a wh— I couldn't even bring myself to think the word, let alone say it aloud. Which was my own damn fault. I didn't have to make her such an indecent proposal. I could have walked up to her like a normal person and told her how I felt. How I'd *always* felt.

But no.

Although I *could* have done that, I knew it wasn't enough. Not for Abigail.

I needed to show her exactly how I felt. Exactly how I had always felt. And with any luck—no! Screw luck—it would take effort, and I was willing to put in all the effort in the world to show Abigail Blakely how much I loved her, always had and always would.

I slipped out of the house and headed to the office long before the sun came up. By sheer force of will, I managed to stay away most of the day. Not that I was able to get any actual work done. Not with the lure of the security cameras that were all over my home. I tried not to, but I couldn't seem to stop myself from powering up the app and checking the cameras at my house, and most importantly, the reward that was on the other end.

And she knew it.

There was zero doubt in my mind that Abigail knew I was watching her. She wasn't stupid. She knew there were cameras all over the house. She used to tease me about it.

"You live alone," she'd said the first time I'd shown her the system on my computer. "Who are you watching? Poor Mrs. Mclean?"

She'd laughed, but I knew it was in good fun. And she was right. It's not like I was watching anyone, because there was no one to watch. Truthfully, I'd used my house as a testing ground for any new systems and cameras. And more than that, I missed the excitement and challenge of setting up the security systems myself. Once the company got so big that I spent most of my time in the office, there was always part of me that missed being out in the field. Changing out the cameras and systems in my own home allowed me the opportunity to keep my skills up and have a little fun doing it.

"You never know," I'd teased as I wiggled my eyebrows. But

I couldn't keep up the charade, even in fun. I shook my head. "Mostly I just keep them off. Because you're right. There's no one to watch. Maybe I should get cats."

I remembered the entire conversation, even after it dissolved into talk about adopting cats and how many I should have. Abigail had cats growing up, and she'd mentioned how she always wanted one again, but the apartments she was living in wouldn't allow them. We'd only been dating three weeks at that point, way too early to adopt a pet together.

But maybe one day.

We'd never gotten to that day.

The memory evaporated and all of my attention was redirected to the screen in front of me, where Abigail had moved out to the pool deck. She shrugged out of the robe she was wearing and let it fall to the ground at her feet, revealing her deliciously curvy body clad in only the ridiculously tiny bikini I'd chosen for her. It was a bit skimpier than I thought she might be comfortable with, but truthfully that wasn't why I'd picked it out. It was the print. I'd bought it specifically because it was white with a bold cherry print on it.

She'd remember. I knew it in my heart. Abigail would remember the night we bought a bag of fresh cherries from a roadside stand. We'd laid by the river at the edge of town and eaten every single one of them, sucking the juice from each other's fingers until our stomachs ached from both the laughter and way too much of the delicious fruit.

She'd remember.

My body sprang to life at the sight of her when she faced the direction of the camera and flipped her hair back behind her shoulders.

Damn.

She looked better in the suit than I could even have imagined.

Abigail had sunglasses on, but I didn't miss the smirk on her lips as she grabbed the bottle of sun lotion, turned, and bent over as she slowly, torturously started applying it. She took her time rubbing the lotion all over every inch of her body and when she was done, she turned, once more tossed her hair from her shoulders, and winked directly into the camera.

I couldn't help but chuckle and fall for her a bit more. Any other woman would have run off after a scene like the night before, but not Abigail. She wasn't like other women. She was so much stronger, and she still had that fire in her that had been there all those years ago.

As tempting as it would be to watch her, I wanted to give her the privacy she deserved. Besides, I would never make it through the day with her distracting me.

As it turned out, I still didn't get any work done. I also wasn't able to put her out of my head. Not even for a second. Maybe having her in my home wasn't a good idea after all.

What if she didn't feel the same as me after all this time?

Sex was one thing. But I wanted more. I *needed* more from her. I always had.

I hated feeling insecure, about anything. And I *never* did. Except when it came to Abigail. She was my kryptonite. Always had been.

Somehow I managed to get through the day and left the office behind. There was no sign of Abigail when I arrived home, but I hadn't expected to see her. Not really. She'd be getting ready for the party. I went directly to my suite and took my time showering, shaving, and dressing in the custom tailored tuxedo.

I took one last look in the mirror at my reflection and took a deep breath. Tonight at the club would either make or break everything. I couldn't wait much longer to tell her the truth, and I wasn't sure how she would react. I needed to be prepared for her to walk away. This time forever.

I spent most of the day at the pool, letting the warm sun lull me into a deep relaxation before diving into the water to cool off. When I'd had enough of lounging, I'd gone for a little walk through the gardens behind the house. I'd always loved Phillip's gardens. His house could feel cold and empty at times, but the garden was always welcoming and full of life. In the few short months we were together, Phillip and I spent a lot of time out there.

Including the night I met the man who would become my husband.

I stopped short as I walked into the small clearing where we'd had that picnic. The picnic I'd been so sure would be a turning point in our relationship.

Well, it had. I snorted a little and shook my head.

Just not in the way I wanted it to be.

Our day had been lovely, and the picnic Phillip had prepared for us—or had Mrs. Mclean prepare for us—was delicious. The wine was sweet and despite the lingering worry I had about the way Phillip had turned me down sexually the night before, everything was perfect.

"Abigail?" I'd just taken a bite of a cracker that I swallowed quickly with a sip of wine before I took his hand. He looked so serious, so I'd given him my most encouraging smile before he continued. "These last few months with you have been... well..." He shook his head and laughed a little. He was usually so confident, something about the way he'd tripped over his words was unsettling.

He swallowed and stroked the back of my hand with his

thumb as he looked in my eyes. I tried and failed to figure out what was going on behind his own dark gaze. "Every moment I spend with you is so much fun and we laugh, and…well, I've never laughed like I have with you."

He was breaking up with me. I was so sure of it. Sure, we had fun and we laughed. But that was it. And was it enough? I didn't think so. How could it be? I tried, but failed to keep the smile on my face as worry filled me. "But it's more than just fun." He said the word clumsily, as if it were an afterthought. I barely heard him as he continued, "I know you've been wanting to take things to the next—"

"Phillip." I cut him off and yanked my hand away. If there was going to be any chance at saving things with him, I needed to explain myself and how attracted I was to him. He'd been holding off on taking things to the next level, but I was sure and I didn't want to wait. I hoped like hell it didn't scare him off. "I wasn't trying to come on so strong. I was just—"

"No!" He interrupted me and grabbed my hand back. "I liked it. I just…"

"Look, Phillip." I blinked back hot tears, looked down at the blanket, and started picking at a loose string. "I get it. I just—"

"No." He shook my hand in his, and I finally looked up at his handsome face, twisted in concern. "Abigail, it's not that," he said. "I wanted to take things slow because…" He sucked in a breath and then everything changed.

"I love you."

"Hey! There you are!"

A man I'd never seen burst from the bushes, drowning out Phillip's words. Words I wasn't sure I'd heard correctly, but really, really hoped I had.

The man slapped Phillip on the back and pulled him up

73

away from me into a hug. "Thought you might be waiting to pick me up at the airport, Phil!"

"I didn't know you were coming back today, Daniel. I—"

"And *who* is this?"

The newcomer pushed Phillip aside and knelt in front of me. "You are gorgeous." He took my hand and pressed his lips to it. There was something about the way he looked at me, the way his eyes seemed to see right through me. My cheeks burned from the attention, and I looked to Phillip for help out of the awkward situation. His arms were crossed tightly over his chest, his lips pressed into a line and a look of cold indifference on his face. And that's when I knew I must have heard him wrong only a few moments before. Because how could he tell me he loved me and then, only moments later, look at me that way?

That was the day everything changed. Daniel was an almost constant presence in our lives, when he returned. For a while, it was always the three of us, but Phillip pulled away quickly. His excuses were fast and frequent as to why he couldn't join us when we went out. "You go with Daniel. It's fine. No. I don't mind. Have fun. Maybe you should let Daniel take you to the dance."

Looking back, it happened so smoothly. I'd been dating Phillip, and so sure I'd been in love, and then…I was with Daniel.

Not only had Phillip *not* fought for me, he'd more or less handed me to Daniel.

I was surprised to feel the sting of the betrayal as keenly as if it had just happened. I thought I was long over it. After all, I'd made my choice, too.

I took another deep breath as I looked over the grassy clearing where everything had changed, and spun on my heel.

I had a party to get ready for.

Chapter Eight

THERE WAS ONLY one dress hanging in the closet that would be suitable for a function at the pretentious country club. Aspen Valley might be a small town in a valley at the edge of the mountains, but that didn't stop the members of the club from behaving as if they were very important.

And, to be fair, they were.

Well, they might not be important, but they were rich. Aspen Valley was known for being full of millionaires, and more and more billionaires. With the hot summers and mild winters, even at the edge of the mountains, it was a little pocket of paradise for the wealthy to golf, entertain, and show off their money on the lake with their ridiculous boats.

They also liked to regularly parade their wealth at the country club with these stupid parties that, up until recently, I'd also been a usual participant in. But I'd never been comfortable with them. Unlike most of the club members, I hadn't come from money. I was raised simply as an "other" in Aspen Valley. Until the year I met Phillip, and then subsequently Daniel, I'd been sure I would follow a similar path as my friends: college and a job, or married with children, working a modest job that supported the rich residents. Never in a million years had I thought I would ever be one of *them*.

And now I wasn't.

I spun in the mirror and took in the length of the blue, shiny dress. It was slit high on my thigh, just short of scandalous. The fabric hugged my body in the most flattering way, pushing my breasts up and together, in a way that I knew would have more than one tongue wagging.

I loved it.

But would Phillip?

Presumably, he'd chosen it for me. But had he been thinking of my twenty-something body? I wasn't the same young woman I'd been when we'd dated. Time changed things. I turned and examined my breasts. Sure, they were pushed up and perky in the dress, but in real life…there was definitely a little more sagging and a few wrinkles where there hadn't been before. I'd never had children—more of Daniel's decision than my own—so I'd never had to deal with the way bearing children ultimately changed a woman. But still, time changed things. *Would Phillip still like what he saw?*

I trembled at the thought, but it wasn't only that. After leaving things the way we did the night before, would he… well…did he still want me there? And why? So many questions, and I sure hoped I would finally get some answers, either way.

With one more quick look in the mirror, I checked my hair, that I had left in soft curls hanging over my shoulders, and my makeup, which I'd done with strong, slightly winged eyeliner, shimmery shadow to match my dress and dark lashes, choosing to leave my lips natural.

The rejection from the night before still stung, but when I walked down the hall into the foyer where Phillip was waiting for me, looking like some sort of *GQ* model in his tux, my heart stopped and did a little flutter in my chest before starting up again.

My entire body tingled, but somehow I managed to continue walking, putting one foot in front of the other.

Even from a distance, I could see his nostrils flare and his eyes darken. He liked what he saw.

Yes. There was definitely something going on with him. How could he push me away one moment, but look like he could eat me up the next?

It didn't make sense. Especially considering he was behaving as if nothing had happened between us the night before. As if I hadn't thrown myself at him. As if we hadn't shared the most passionate kiss I'd ever had. As if he hadn't wanted me as badly as I wanted him. As if he hadn't pushed me away.

Just the same way he'd pretended he hadn't told me he loved me.

No. I chastised myself quickly. *This wasn't the same.*

Phillip flashed his sexy smile at me. "You look ravishing." He held a hand out for me, which I took.

I tried to ignore the spark that rushed through me and settled heavy between my legs as he pulled me close and gave me a chaste kiss on the cheek.

"Ravishing?" I teased. "Interesting choice."

"There really is no other word to describe you, Abigail." Phillip looked at me seriously. "Are we…are we okay?"

His vulnerability softened any leftover tension from the night before. I nodded. "For now."

"I'll take it." His handsome grin once more slid over his face. "Are you ready for this? For these people? There will be questions."

"I'm counting on it."

I definitely sounded much more confident than I felt. We

were quiet on the limo ride to the club. I kept my focus on the lights beyond the window as we made the quick drive. Even without such a striking dress, I knew all eyes would be on me. I was prepared for it. And I could handle it. At least I hoped I could.

Despite my attempt at confidence earlier, I felt like I might throw up, or maybe pass out, as we pulled up to the curved marble staircase and the valet opened the door. I hesitated before taking the young man's offer of assistance. For a moment, I considered what would happen if I just stayed in the car.

Surely we could just turn around and go home. Phillip had already said he wouldn't hold me to the deal. I was free to leave. But that's not why I was there. Not anymore. It was about more than Phillip's indecent proposal, and we both knew it.

He was offering me a chance of redemption with these people. A chance to hold my head up high and face the gossip and the whispers. To show them that I was Abigail Blakely, and I was not the villain they made me out to be. That they *wanted* me to be.

Phillip's hand, strong and reassuring, splayed across my low back. He leaned across the leather seat and gently brushed a curl off my shoulder. "You've got this, Abigail. You are the strongest woman I know. And I'll be right there with you. I won't leave your side."

His words sent a thread of courage through me. He was right—I was strong. I *could* do this. But sometimes even the strongest woman needed help, and that was what he was offering me now.

I leaned back into his touch, but just a little, before I exhaled the breath I was holding. I nodded and accepted the hand of the valet and stepped out into the cool evening air.

He was at my side in an instant, his hand returned to its place on my low back. A few people glanced in our direction, but it was nothing compared to what we faced through the massive double doors.

Together, we walked up the steps and the doormen pulled the huge doors open for our entrance. Instead of marching directly into the lion's den, Phillip paused. He bent down, just a little since the outrageously high heels I wore made me much taller. "You have no reason to be nervous." His voice soothed me. "Every woman in this room wants to be you, and every single man…they want to be *with* you." A shiver ran through me, but it quickly turned to heat, when Phillip added, "But tonight, Abigail, you are all mine."

His words had their desired effect on me as we strode into the ostentatious entryway of what should have been a simple golf club. Nothing was simple in Aspen Valley. I relinquished my thin wrap to the coat check girl—a young lady I'd very recently shared a coffee break with on one of my last shifts. Her mouth briefly fell open in surprise, but I gave her a small smile and a wink.

Without my cover, I felt more exposed in the daring dress. But when I turned back to him, Phillip had nothing but admiration and heat in his gaze. "Have I told you yet how stunning you are?" he asked as I rejoined him.

"I believe the word was *ravishing*." The flirting came naturally, as did the way I let him guide me into the room, his hand once more on my low back. This time, on my exposed bare skin, I felt his heat acutely.

I'd been counting on everyone watching me and judging me. The questions, the whispers, the gossip, certainly. But I had completely underestimated how hard it would be to set foot into the club as a guest after everything that had happened. Working in the pro shop, I'd steeled myself to be *less than*. But this was different. And I especially hadn't counted on how difficult it would be to be there as the guest of Phillip Conrad.

Never mind how hard it was to actually *be* with Phillip. To have his hand on my back, guiding me through the room, his arm around my waist holding me close, almost possessively as we made small talk with the other club members. My entire body was on alert. Every nerve ending acutely aware of his proximity and how good it felt to be with him. Even if it wasn't real.

Together, we fielded inquiries from nosy members.

"Interesting to see you together. Are you…"

"Enjoying our evening?" Phillip would say, playing dumb. "Absolutely. And doesn't Abigail look *ravishing?*"

"We didn't expect to see you—"

"Looking so *ravishing?*"

I had to bite back laughter every time he used the word. Phillip did his best to work it into every conversation, which only made me giggle harder. Which was probably his intention because as the evening wore on, I began to relax.

It felt good—really good—to have the most successful, gorgeous man in the club with all of his attention focused on me in a room full of people who wanted to see me fail.

For a few moments, I could almost forget that the last time I'd been at an event in that very same room had been only weeks before the FBI had crashed through the front door of my home and arrested Daniel for embezzlement. Looking back, Daniel must have known the authorities were closing in on him.

Still, as if nothing were wrong, he held court at the club as if he were the king, with his minions all around him. Men he called friends, but had been secretly stealing from. As he usually did, Daniel completely ignored me the moment we walked through the doors. Leaving me to do my *job.* Which was to be the most popular woman in the room. Years earlier, Daniel had impressed upon me the importance of having the wives of his *colleagues* look up to me. To be sure I was invited to all of the most important events and parties. Never excluded from any of the luncheons or charity events the other wives were hosting. For way too long, I kept my true feelings about the shallow, mindless women I spent my days with hidden. Keep the peace, and play nice. That was my job.

There was a time I felt my role was important. Now, I was disgusted by that version of myself and how naive I had been about it all.

I tried my best to push the past out of my thoughts as I smiled politely and let Phillip do most of the talking. After all, what could I possibly say to these people that wouldn't get me fired? And despite the fact the dress and shoes I currently wore cost more than a month's rent at my apartment, I still needed that job come Monday morning. That hadn't changed.

There was no telling what I might say, especially after a few glasses of champagne. It was easier to stay quiet, making my thoughts known with a few pointed looks before Phillip swept me away to say hello to someone else.

Finally, I'd hit my limit, and I needed a break. There was only so much small talk I could make. But trying my best to be civil to people who didn't deserve it wasn't nearly as exhausting as being with Phillip and the shots of desire that were continuously running through me whenever his fingers traced my arm, his hand pressed against my back, he pulled me close, or just looked at me with those dark eyes of his. I wasn't lying when I told him we were okay, but I still needed answers from him. I just wasn't yet one hundred percent sure of the questions yet. And the longer the night went on, the harder those questions were to formulate.

I excused myself to the ladies' room, which was, mercifully, empty. I quickly locked myself into a stall and whipped out my cell phone from the tiny clutch I carried.

Everything felt so surreal. Being at the club. Phillip. The feelings crashing through me. It was a lot. I needed to touch base with reality.

This is crazy. I quickly texted the group chat. *What am I doing here? With him?*

It only took a second before a reply appeared. Jessie. *I can't imagine how weird it is. Take a breath.*

I nodded. I could almost see her reassuring smile. I did as she suggested and inhaled deeply.

Are they being terrible?

I wasn't surprised that it was Sandy who cared to ask about the other women. I shrugged a little because shockingly, they hadn't been terrible. At least not to my face.

Not as bad as I expected.

How's Phillip?

It was Britt who asked.

Before I could reply, Darla chimed in. *Sexy as hell, I bet.*

I couldn't help but laugh a little as I typed my reply. *Definitely! Also...I don't know...being with him feels...*

I chickened out. I still couldn't tell my best friends that, despite everything, I was still in love with the man.

Don't overthink it, Abby. Your heart knows what to do.

I blinked twice at Sandy's comment. I was positive she disapproved of the very fact that I had accepted Phillip's *deal* at all.

And remember, Jessie's text followed, *this is supposed to be fun.*

Darla's text came quick. *I'm sure Phillip could be all kinds of fun.* Followed by a winky face emoji.

I bit back a laugh. But before I could reply, the bathroom door opened, and I heard voices. I quickly texted my goodbye to the group chat, promising updates when I could manage them, and tucked my phone away as I heard a familiar nasally voice say, "Can you even believe the nerve of her to show up here?"

Janine Lister. Inwardly, I groaned.

"Right? And looking like...*that. I mean, that dress. It's hardly appropriate for the club.*" Another voice I vaguely recognized as Bitsy Neville chimed in.

I rolled my eyes because I knew perfectly well that Bitsy was just jealous. She couldn't eat a grape without gaining five pounds. Even when we were *friends,* she'd constantly made snide comments about my form-fitting clothing choices. Pure jealousy.

"And with *Phillip Conrad.*" Janine's voice was thick with malice. "Do you think they've been sleeping together all these years?"

I bristled, but stayed put.

"Definitely," Bitsy agreed. "It's no secret that Phillip's been desperately in love with her forever."

It wasn't?

"But don't you think it's kind of pathetic?" Bitsy continued. "To take her back after she jumped into Daniel's bed all those years ago and then paraded it in front of him all this time?"

"So pathetic," Janine agreed.

Phillip was anything but pathetic. But these women... My hands clenched into fists, but still I didn't move. I wouldn't gain anything by—

"And to bring her *here* of all places?" Janine scoffed. "After she stole all our money."

I had nothing to do with their money. Logically, I knew I should just stay quiet and let them gossip. But that was *logic,* and I was having a harder and harder time seeing how it might apply to me anymore. Especially because that was what the old

Abby would do. She wouldn't say anything, afraid to rock the boat or make things hard for Daniel.

"I bet Phillip was in on it, too," Bitsy said. "And then Abby gets a job here, at the club of all places."

What? Did they seriously think I wanted to work here? That it wasn't sheer torture for me every single day?

"It's just like her to keep the spotlight on her. Playing the poor victim is all part of the plan."

I took a deep breath and filled my lungs while the lessons from my past played on repeat in my head. *Be the good wife. Swallow it and stay quiet. Make sure everyone likes you.*

Screw that.

I pushed the stall door open and stepped from the stall. I made eye contact first with Janine, and then Bitsy, in the mirror, a tight smile on my face. "Hi there, ladies." The shock of their over-botoxed, nipped and tucked plastic faces was almost reward enough for having to listen to their vitriol as long as I did. "Sounds like you're having a pretty exciting night." Confidently, I stepped between them to the sink, where I washed my hands slowly and dried them with one of the provided plush hand towels.

Both Janine and Bitsy stepped back from the counter and watched, open-mouthed, but silent until I was done.

I tossed my hair back and straightened as I turned to face them. I looked each of them in the eye and smiled as sweetly as I could.

"Abby!" Bitsy tried and failed to sound sincerely happy to see me.

Way too little. Way too late.

I ignored her. "I'm glad that Phillip and I can provide you with something to talk about in your boring, empty lives."

Janine's mouth opened and shut like a dying fish, but she couldn't seem to find anything to say.

"It must be so tedious to have nothing of interest going on in your own lives."

"Abby," Bitsy spoke once again, "I just wanted to say how nice it is to see you again. You look great."

"Oh?" I chuckled without humor. "Bitsy, I *know* I look great." I stuck my tits out as a reminder that I'd just heard everything she'd said. "But I need to tell you," I added. "Green is not your color." She was wearing a black dress, but the dig wasn't wasted on her. "It really shows your age, and your character."

It was her turn to open and shut her mouth. Bitsy crossed her arms over her chest and grunted.

That was my cue to leave.

"Anyway." I smiled sweetly and made my way toward the door. "Have a great night, ladies. I wouldn't want to leave Phillip waiting." I paused and looked over my shoulder at them. "After all, spending my time gossiping in the bathroom when I could be spending time with the sexiest, most successful man in the room, truly *would* be pathetic, wouldn't it?"

I managed to exit the bathroom with my head held high and without stumbling over my feet. The second the door swung shut behind me and I was alone in the hall, I took a deep, gulping breath and willed my heart to stop racing. I did my best to put on a strong front, and I was pretty sure I'd succeeded, but I was rapidly hitting my limit. I didn't know how much more of any of this I could take.

Chapter Nine

EVERY MOMENT ABIGAIL was gone from my side, I felt her absence acutely. I'd waited a very long time to spend an evening with her, and despite how I'd managed to get her here, she was here. With me. I knew it was hard on her to be there after everything, and with a beautiful smile on her face that must have been sheer torture. But she'd handled herself like the queen she was.

I stood next to the bar, where I could keep an eye on the hallway where she'd disappeared to go to the ladies' room. Not that I thought she would try to slip out the back. As tempted as Abigail might be to escape this evening, I didn't think she would.

It was hard on her, sure. But there was something else. Something between us. Just like I had every other minute for the last twenty-four hours, I replayed every second of the kiss we'd shared the night before. It had been so much more than just a kiss. There were feelings there that couldn't be denied. By either of us. And I'd be dammed if I let even one more night go by without getting to the bottom of it. It was time. It was *way* past time. We just needed to get through the party. It was more important than even Abigail realized.

I glanced again toward the hallway but there was still no sign of her. I tossed the rest of my whiskey back, slammed the glass on the bar, and was just about to go in search of her when I was stopped.

"Phillip Conrad."

Anyone else and I would have immediately excused myself. But when I turned and saw the face of my old college roommate, my face split into a smile.

"Trent Thomas. What are you doing here?" I took his hand and pulled him into a back-slapping man hug. "It's been what? Twenty years?"

"At least." He grinned. "I'm in town working on a big acquisition. There's a lot of opportunity out West. I was told this was the place to be tonight." He turned to survey the room and I let my eyes follow his, seeing what he was seeing. A bunch of self-important men and women trying to make themselves even more important. It was stupid. All of it.

"If this is what passes for entertainment in Aspen Valley, I may have to rethink my decision." He tipped his glass to his lips and grinned. "Or at least go out and find my own, if you know what I mean?"

"I'd say that's probably a better option, buddy." I chuckled. "It's good to see you, man. I wish I'd known you were coming to town. We could…" My thought drifted away as I once again looked toward the hallway. "Sorry, what brings you to town?"

"I'm always on the lookout for a good development opportunity and frankly, I've been looking for a change. So here I am, and…" Trent laughed as I once more let my gaze drift toward the hallway where Abigail should have already reappeared. "I'd say you have more important things going on than worrying about why I'm in town."

I'd always liked Trent and in only a few minutes of seeing him again, I remembered why. He was easy to get along with, but at the same time, he was a sharp, and almost ruthless businessman. Last I'd heard, he ran a very successful property development firm. He seemed to have a knack in seeing an opportunity where others simply saw barren land or dilapidated buildings. He always had been a sharp man.

I shook my head. "I would like to catch up," I said apologetically. "You'll be in town for a bit?"

"If all goes well, I will."

I laughed. "I'm sure it will." I was already starting to break away. "I'm really sorry, I just—"

"Forget about it." Trent slapped me on the back. "I see Shane Grant over there, anyway," he said. "I need to talk to him about some office space he was going to loan me while I'm in town."

Trent said something else, but I'd already stopped listening. Abigail had finally reappeared.

And something was wrong.

I saw it the moment Abigail stepped back into the ballroom.

Something had happened.

I grabbed a glass of champagne from a nearby waiter and went directly to her.

As if it were the most natural thing in the world—which it felt like—I slipped my arm around her waist and handed her the glass as I spoke into her ear. "You look like you could use this."

Her smile was weak, but she hid it with a sip from the glass.

She trembled ever so slightly in my arms as I held her fast. Whatever had happened, it had definitely shaken her. But she was working hard not to let it show. It was just one of the things I loved about her. She was so damn strong.

Abigail had every reason not to walk into the club with me, especially after the way I'd pushed her away the night before, but she had. With her head held high. She was amazing and courageous. Even if she was having a moment right now, I was already so proud of her for coming this far with me. She didn't even know how badly she needed this redemption. How important it was to show those assholes that she could not be broken and she was not the sleaze ball that her ex-husband was. She deserved that, and so much more. She never would have given herself the opportunity to do this on her own. I knew that. Which was why I'd pushed her into it. One of the reasons.

The other was purely selfish.

"Thank you." She handed me the empty glass back. "Can we go now?" She glanced around, and froze. I watched as her face transformed into a mask of defiance when she saw something over my shoulder.

Slowly, with my arm still wrapped possessively around her, I turned to see Janine Lister and Bitsy Neville emerge from the hallway and the ladies' room where Abigail had just returned from. And it all made sense.

Dammit. I didn't doubt for a second that Abigail could hold her own, but I also knew there was always a limit to what one person should have to bear. I feared I'd pushed Abigail right up against that limit.

"Those women." I spoke under my breath. "Did they—"

"It doesn't matter." She fluffed her hair in an effort to appear unaffected.

But I knew exactly what had happened. There'd been a confrontation, as I knew there would have had to be, and Abigail had no doubt handled herself like the warrior she was. But even a warrior needed a little help sometimes.

"How does that song go?" I grinned, as an idea that would achieve more than one thing formed in my head.

She turned toward me and tilted her head in question so her hair cascaded over her bare shoulder enticingly.

"Let's give them something to talk about."

Before she could reply, I moved my hand from her waist to the small of her back so I could lead her directly to the center of the dance floor, where I pulled her scandalously close. Air escaped from her lungs with a puff as her breasts pressed into my chest. My cock thickened in my pants, but I needed to focus.

The music started, and I moved her effortlessly with the beat. We'd only danced together on a few occasions, and even though it had been many years since I held her in my arms, my body remembered hers, and hers, mine.

For the next few songs, I spun, dipped, and danced with my gorgeous date in a way that was certain to have every eye in the place on us. Not that I knew for sure, because I never once took my eyes off hers. And why would I? She was the most beautiful woman in the room. And ultimately, there was no one else who mattered to me the way she did. Not. Even. Close.

The only thing that mattered in that moment was the woman in my arms, and making sure she felt every bit the goddess she was.

When finally the band started to play a slow song, I pulled Abigail even closer, and slid my hand lower down her back until it rested just over the swell of her ass. I took a moment to let us each catch our breath. "Feel better?"

She smiled, but it didn't quite reach her eyes. "A little."

"Do I have more work to do?" I teased. "I could spin you a little—"

"Why are we here, Phillip?" There was a tinge of sadness

in her voice, and I hated that I might have had even the slightest part to play in putting it there.

Her question caught me off guard and I stumbled. But only a little.

I had a choice. I could give her the glib response. The easy answer. The one that suggested she was here because she *owed* me. But we both knew that wasn't true.

We both knew it last night in my office when my lips were on hers, my hands all over her, my need for her almost completely out of control. There was no more pretending.

No more hiding. But still...

"Why do you think you're here?"

Abigail pulled away a little, but didn't hesitate with her answer. "Honestly? I'm not sure. At first I thought it might be some kind of a twisted game you were playing, but that's not who you are."

I shook my head. "No." I continued to lead her slowly in the dance.

"And then I thought that maybe it was so I could..." She glanced toward the hallway before looking back at me. She swallowed hard. "So I could get some sort of revenge."

"Not revenge, Abigail. That's not your style. Or mine."

Her head moved slightly in agreement. "You're right. Not revenge, but..."

"Redemption," I supplied for her.

Her beautiful eyes widened in understanding.

"You never deserved the way these people made you feel," I continued. "I needed you to see that."

She was quiet for a moment, her eyes dropping to the ground before she once more looked up at me. "Thank you," she said softly. "But that's not everything, is it?"

I shook my head.

"Why am I *really* here, Phillip?"

For the first time that I could remember, Abigail looked vulnerable and unsure. It took the breath from my lungs.

"I thought I knew, but…I'm so confused, Phillip." Her feet stopped and we stood, unmoving, in the middle of the dance floor. "I thought maybe you felt…that there was something… but last night, you—"

"Knew you deserved so much more."

She pulled away. "That doesn't make sense."

She was too far away. I needed her close. I reached out and once more slid my arm around her waist and pressed my hand to her back. I needed to touch her. "It makes perfect sense, Abigail," I murmured in her ear as I pulled her in to me again. With my free hand, I tilted her chin up to look at me. "You deserve so much more than a quick fuck on top of my desk." I felt her startle in my arms at my brash language. Good. I liked to keep her guessing. "*So* much. You deserve to be loved and cherished and…" I swallowed hard and made sure she was listening carefully, because I could only say it once. "You deserve the truth, Abigail."

"The truth?"

I nodded slightly, but didn't hesitate or stumble over the words I'd been waiting far too long to say. I'd said them one other time, a long time ago, but this time I was going to make damn sure she heard me and there was no mistaking exactly how I felt. "The truth is, I love you, Abigail. I always have." I didn't wait for my words to sink in. Instead, I pressed my lips to hers and kissed her. Because it was the only other thing I could think to do.

He loved me.
He always had.

Two thoughts replayed over and over in my head on high speed until I felt like the room was spinning around me. But it didn't matter, because Phillip was kissing me. Right there in the middle of the ballroom, with everyone watching. Right out in the open. As if it didn't matter.

As if *they* didn't matter.

As if I was the only thing that mattered. Because he loved me.

He. Loved. Me.

It took me a few seconds to catch up to what was happening, but when I did, my entire body responded to him. I pressed closer to him, if it were even possible, and let his mouth consume mine. His hand left my chin and twisted through my hair, holding my head in place—as if I would go anywhere.

Never again.

I'd walked away from this man once and it turned out to be the biggest mistake of my life. I wouldn't do it again. But then again, he'd let me go first. He'd said those words once before and then…

I pulled away from the kiss, but just a little. "Why?" It was an incomplete question. I swallowed hard, and tried again. "All those years ago…" I started and saw the realization flash in his eyes. "Why did you walk away?"

He squeezed his eyes shut for a second, as if it were painful to hear the question, but he was still listening.

"If you loved me then, why didn't you fight for me?"

It was a question I'd wanted to ask for years, certainly, but even I don't think I realized I needed the answer as much as I did. But when Phillip opened his eyes and looked deep into mine, I knew how badly I needed to hear his explanation.

With his arms still wrapped tight around me, he said, "It

was the biggest mistake of my life, Abigail. I've regretted it every single day since."

"That's not an answer."

"I know," he admitted. "I don't have an answer that is worthy of you." He dipped his head a little. "Because *I* wasn't worthy of you. Not then." His words caused a stab of physical pain, but I forced myself to hear him out. "I'm ashamed to say I was scared. I'd just professed my love and then Daniel swept in. You have to understand. Daniel always got what he wanted. Ever since we were boys. And he wanted you." He shook his head a little. "I just assumed he'd get you, too. Once he set his sights on you, I knew it was only a matter of time."

"That's not true."

"Isn't it?"

He raised his eyebrows, and anger flared through me. I jerked away from his grasp, not caring that we were still in the middle of the dance floor. I didn't care who heard us. And I certainly didn't give a damn about what any of these people thought about me or my life. Not anymore.

"No! It's not true at all." I wrapped my arms around my waist to keep from shaking. "You'd just told me you loved me."

"And you didn't say it back."

My mouth fell open. "I was caught off guard, Phillip. Daniel was there and so much happened all at once. I didn't have a chance to say anything, let alone that I loved you, too."

I watched his face soften.

"You loved me?"

"For such a smart man, you can be so fucking stupid, Phillip." I threw up my hands and turned to leave, but he caught my hand in his and stopped me. Still, I didn't turn around.

"I know," he said quietly. "Letting you walk away from me was the biggest fucking mistake of my life." He squeezed my hand a little, and I could feel the build-up of tension in my body slowly start to dissipate. I turned to face him once again. The pain he felt was etched in his face like a mask. "I should have fought for you. I never should have let Daniel push his way in. More than anything, I wanted to race to the ends of the earth to win you back. But I couldn't."

"Yes," I said simply. "You could have."

"No." He offered me a small smile. "I wasn't worthy of you. You deserved a man who would never have let you go. A man who was strong enough to fight for you instead of standing by like a loser. A man who wouldn't let anything or anyone stand between you and him. I wasn't that man. So, I let you go."

Damn.

But Phillip wasn't done. "I have spent the last fifteen years working to be the man who is worthy of you, Abigail." He slipped his hand down my curves until his fingers were splayed over my hip. "I would slay dragons for you, and that includes anyone in this room." He smirked, and I burst out laughing at the idea of Janine and Bitsy as dragons. It wasn't far off. "I would do anything for you," he said, cutting off my laughter with his intensity. "I have never stopped loving you. I just hope like hell you feel the same way about me, and…"

"And what?" I tipped my head and bit my bottom lip a little, causing him to emit a low groan only I could hear.

"Judging by the way you kissed me, I'm going to go out on a limb and say that you feel exactly the same way."

Damn, he was cocky.

But he was right.

One hundred percent.

I leaned in until my breasts were pressed up against his chest, and I whispered in his ear. "I think we are very overdue in showing each other exactly how we really feel, don't you?"

He tightened his grip on me and groaned in reply, so I added, "Take me home, Phillip."

He moved so quickly that if he didn't have a firm grip on me, I might have stumbled. As it was, it didn't matter because he scooped me up effortlessly into his arms and once more kissed me until my breath came hard and fast. And then, as if it were the most natural thing in the world, he walked swiftly across the dance floor, past the gawking faces and murmured gossip that I couldn't have cared less about, out the front door and into the waiting car.

Chapter Ten

THE CAR RIDE, short as it was, was sheer torture. The fact that I somehow had managed to wait until we'd finally made it home from the club and walked through the front door of my mansion before I stripped Abigail naked of that sinfully gorgeous blue dress she wore was a testament to the control and willpower I'd cultivated over the years of watching the love of my life from afar.

But the moment the door closed behind us, I had her pressed up against the solid oak door, my mouth on hers, and my hands everywhere.

I pressed one hand against the wall, bracing myself against her. The moan that slipped from her throat as I slid my hand up her side and cupped her breast through the silky dress almost tore the last shred of self-control I still had.

The dress was almost tissue-thin but it was still too much between us. I needed her bare. Immediately.

My hands found the zipper on her back and tugged, but it wouldn't move. A growl ripped from my throat as I tried again.

Nothing.

"Here, I'll…" Abigail shimmied to the side in an effort to help, but I was far too impatient.

"No time." The words were a growl as I gripped the edge of the dress and pulled. The silky fabric tore away easily and she gasped.

"Phillip, the—"

"It's just a dress." I groaned as I was finally able to take a good look at her free of the garment. "I'll buy you another one. Hell, I'll buy you a hundred—" The words died on my lips as I took in the sight of her.

Speechless was an understatement. My mind went completely blank at the gorgeous woman in front of me. The world around me blurred. There was only Abigail.

Yes, I'd seen her before. Hell, the bathing suit she'd been wearing earlier had less material than the black lacy bra and panties she currently had on. The corset she'd worn the night in my office had been sinfully sexy, of course. But this…

Damn.

There was literally nothing in the world that compared to the pure beauty of the woman I was desperately in love with standing before me, her skin flushed with passion, her breasts heaving with every breath, her lips parted just a little, yearning for another kiss…*fuck.*

I licked my lips and took in a deep breath, trying to give myself just one more moment to look at her like this. Drink in the sight of her. Every. Single. Inch.

"Phillip?"

I didn't answer. Instead, I let my gaze travel slowly up the length of her. She still wore her heels, the dress—in shreds—a pool of blue silk at her feet. Her legs were lean and long, leading to curvy hips that begged to be held. But her sinful curves didn't end there. Hell, they were only just beginning. Her breasts, round and full, were the perfect size. She was every bit as gorgeous as she'd ever been. More so. If it were even possible, time had only made her more beautiful. My fingers flexed with the need to caress her. Finally, I allowed my eyes to lock on hers. Her pupils were dilated with desire as she leaned back against the wall seductively.

She crooked a finger and beckoned me to her.

Before I went to her, I shed my jacket and tie, dropping them to the floor before I slowly unbuttoned my tuxedo vest and stepped toward her. I was done waiting. So. Very. Done.

I pulled Abigail toward me and kissed her until her knees buckled a little, but I held her fast. She wasn't getting away from me again. Never again.

And finally, we were going to consummate our relationship the way we should have all those years ago.

"I want to take my time with you, Abigail." My words were rough against her neck as my kisses traveled lower. I needed to taste all of her. I needed every part of her.

She groaned as my fingers tore at her bra, leaving it too in tatters so I could finally have access to her breasts. I cupped and kneaded her soft flesh. There was no way I was going to be able to take my time. I needed this woman as badly as I needed air to breathe.

"No," Abigail moaned into my ear.

My hand froze right as my fingers slipped under the elastic of her panties.

No?

I'd stop. I'd walk away again if that's what she wanted. It might kill me, but I would.

I shifted so I could look in her eyes. "You want me to stop?"

Her face transformed immediately. Her mouth opened and her eyes widened. "No! I mean, no. Don't stop. And for the love of God, do *not* take your time with me, Phillip." She grabbed my collar and pulled me to her, hard.

Clarity restored, there was no slowing down. Everything sped up.

Abigail's hands clawed at my clothes, until I too was naked, my impossibly hard erection pressed up against her soft belly as our hands grabbed and slid all over the other as if we needed to relearn each other's bodies, which we did. And at the same time, learn them for the very first time. In the very best way.

"I'm not going to make it to the bedroom, Abigail." With my hand wrapped in her hair, I tipped her head back and bit and sucked at her throat until she squirmed beneath my attentions, her hips thrusting up against me. My free hand slipped between her legs, and she immediately cried out from the attention.

She wasn't going to make it either.

Abigail lifted her head and when our eyes met, I knew it was true. We needed this *now*.

Without another second of hesitation, I scooped her up easily, cupping her ass in my hands. She wrapped her legs around my waist as I pressed her up against the wall.

"Yes, Phillip. Yes." She moaned and arched her back as I lifted her and poised my hard length, ready to finally have what we'd both been wanting and needing for far too long. But I couldn't.

Not yet.

She sensed my hesitation and her eyes opened in question.

"Abigail. I can't do this."

What?

He wasn't doing this again. He wasn't rejecting me again. Leaving me wanting and needing right at the last minute. He couldn't do this. Not now.

Not this time.

My eyes widened.

"Not like this."

I wanted to scream. I wanted to cry. And it wasn't just about sexual frustration. It was so much more.

I needed to get away, but he held me in a way that I couldn't move. I was at his mercy, up against the wall, and his grip on me only tightened.

"Phillip, I—"

"I love you, Abigail."

I froze, more confused than ever.

"And I want this," he continued. "I want *you*."

Frustration flooded through me. We *were* doing this. *What was the problem?*

"I want you, too, Phillip." I tried, again, to wiggle in his grip. "I think that much is clear."

His lips twitched up into a grin. "Wanting is not enough, Abigail. It will never be enough."

"Phillip?"

"I want all of you, Abigail. Or nothing at all. I won't settle for anything less."

This man was going to be the very death of me. I reached out and grabbed his chin in my hand so he was looking me directly in the eye. It was my turn to hold him firm. My breasts rose and fell hard against his chest with every breath I took. "Phillip." I kept my voice level despite the flood of feelings crashing through me, never mind the intense waves of desire that were only barely being held at bay. "I'm only going to say this once, so please listen carefully." I paused and took a quick breath. "You *do* have all of me. I know now that you always have."

I felt every word deep in my heart. The last few days, being with Phillip—no matter how it came to be—had been the greatest gift I could have ever had. And if it meant going through everything I'd gone through with Daniel, and the club, and even the way I'd peeled bills from his money clip that day, I'd do it again. Every. Single. Time.

Phillip's grip on me shifted. But still...he wouldn't give us both what we wanted. What we *needed*.

"It's not enough, Abigail."

I swallowed back a scream. My body ached for him. I needed him like I'd never needed anything or anyone in my whole life. Hot tears built in my eyes. I was going to cry. Oh God, no. I couldn't cry. Not now.

"Phillip." I leaned my face as close as I could to his until our lips almost touched. "I need you. I've always needed you. It's always been you, Phillip. It always will be you." I swallowed hard. "I love you, Phillip."

A combination of a groan and a sob sounded between us. I couldn't be sure of who made the sound, or whether it was a mixture of the two of us—not that it mattered, because a second later, the only thing that mattered was that Phillip had finally, mercifully shifted our bodies and was inside me. His hard length filled me completely and perfectly. Like a puzzle that had finally, after far too long, found its final, missing piece.

I gasped out of relief, need, and...*love* for this man.

I released my grip on his chin so I could hold him closer to me, my palms pressed flat on his smooth back as he thrust deeper inside me.

"I love you, Phillip." Every time the words slipped from my lips, they felt better than the time before. They'd always been there, right on the tip of my tongue but for some reason, I hadn't been able to say them until that moment. But now that I had, I didn't think I'd ever be able to stop. I wanted to tell the world that I loved Phillip Conrad. And I always had.

Phillip groaned; his muscles tightened under my grip and

he increased his pace, kissing me hard until I knew my lips would be bruised. There would be time for exploring each other later, for making love and keeping it slow and tender.

For now, the only thing that mattered was this union that had been far too long in the making.

"Say it again." His voice was gruff as he pulled his lips from mine.

"I love you."

He growled. His hands tightened their grip on my bottom.

"Again."

"I love you." My climax was building within me. Fast. My thighs trembled around him but he didn't relent.

"I love you, Abigail." He caught my mouth with his in another deep kiss and pressed my back harder against the wall.

I tightened my legs around him and matched him thrust for thrust.

"One more time," he demanded.

"I love you, Phillip." The words had barely slipped from my lips when my orgasm crashed through me. I tipped my head back and cried out as Phillip took his own release with a long, low growl.

Chapter Eleven

SOMEHOW WE'D MANAGED to move from the foyer and into the master bedroom, where this time I took my time with Abigail, kissing her, touching her, and exploring every inch of her beautiful body, even more luscious now than when I'd first met her.

And that wasn't the only thing that was different, in all the best ways. I had never doubted my feelings for Abigail. Not one time since I'd realized my terrible mistake and everything I'd lost by letting Daniel sweep her away had my love for her faltered. But now, with her in my arms, her body pressed against mine, I realized how wrong I'd been about that love back then.

Because even though I'd been so sure about my feelings when we were younger, I'd doubted them at the worst possible moment. And that was unforgivable. Yet, at the same time, I wouldn't have changed it, because everything that had happened, all the time and space between us for all those years, they'd only done one thing: strengthened what I felt for her. And she for me.

Now, those feelings were so much bigger than I ever could

have begun to imagine all those years ago. Especially now that I knew without a doubt that she felt the same about me… finally, it was only going to get better. Stronger.

Abigail had fallen asleep at some point after we'd made love again but she stirred now in her sleep. I rolled over on one elbow and watched as her eyelids began to flutter open. The moment she registered me there, watching her, a small smile traveled over her lips.

"So, I wasn't dreaming it?"

I traced a finger up her belly, between her breasts, and bent over to press a tender kiss to her lips. "Wide awake, sweetheart."

"Good." She stretched her arms up over her head and moaned a little. "I'm sore all over." My smile dipped but then she flipped over to her side to face me and grinned. "And I love it."

"You know what I love?"

Her eyes twinkled. "Me?"

"I was going to say breakfast in bed," I teased. "But yes, you." I moved quickly so she was once again flat on her back, only now I was overtop her, caging her in with my arms. "I do love you very much. And I love saying it out loud. Finally." I dropped my head to kiss her slowly. The kiss stirred me to life again. I don't think I would ever tire of her now that I had her. I nudged her legs apart with my knee, and without hesitation, Abigail arched her back up to meet me.

We were the perfect match.

She groaned low and long as I entered her exquisitely slowly this time.

We didn't take our eyes off each other as we made love lazily, barely moving and still half asleep, until our climaxes snuck up on us, curling from our toes until finally they exploded through every cell of our bodies. I kissed her deep, twisting my tongue with hers as we both moaned our mutual release and finally rolled apart.

"Mmm, and I do love doing that." I tucked my hand under the pillow. If I dared touch her again, we'd never leave this bed. Not that there'd be anything wrong with that, but Abigail might want breakfast sooner or later. And she would need to keep her strength up, because all of my plans for the next few days involved her and me, naked, in this bed together.

Right on cue, her stomach growled. Loud.

She laughed. "What was it that you were saying about breakfast?"

Reluctantly, I rolled from the bed to find my phone where I'd left it on the dresser across the room, and text Mrs. Mclean our breakfast order. Not that I would need to. No doubt the woman already had a feast underway. She had a sixth sense about these things.

"And maybe after breakfast," Abigail was talking as I composed my message, "I should probably get going home. I have to take care of—"

"What?" I spun to face her, the breakfast order forgotten. "What did you say?"

"I should probably get home and take care of a few things." Her smile was hesitant and unsure. "I mean, I only planned on being here for the weekend, and I have things I need to take care of. I work in the—"

"No." In two quick strides, I was across the room and sitting on the bed in front of her. "Abigail, no."

"No?" Her voice shook and she straightened her spine. "What do you mean?"

"Did you mean what you said last night?" I was so sure of the answer. I felt it in my bones. But now, with the bright light of the morning, I needed to be sure she'd meant it when she'd said those words. That she hadn't just said them in the passion of the moment. I needed to know without any uncertainty at all that Abigail Blakely loved me. I'd made that mistake once. And it had cost me everything. I wouldn't do it again. "Tell me the truth. Did you mean it?"

"Did I mean it when I told you I loved you?"

I nodded.

"Phillip! How can you even ask me that?"

I saw the indignation in her face, the insult that I even had to ask, but still...I needed to hear the words from her lips. I hated how it must seem. But it wasn't like that. It was...I just needed to know.

"I need to know, Abigail. Did you—"

"Of course I meant it." She shook her head as if she couldn't make sense of me or what I was saying, which was probably fairly accurate. "I love you, Phillip. Don't ever doubt it."

And just like that, I could breathe. My heart started to beat again and once more, blood began to flow through my veins. She loved me. Of course she did. I'd felt it every time we made love. Our connection was deeper than anything I'd ever experienced before, and that could only be love. I dipped my head and shook it, embarrassed by my moment of insecurity.

"And I love you." I lifted my head so our eyes met. "So don't leave."

She laughed a little. "Just because I love you doesn't mean I don't have a life and a—"

"That's what I'm saying." I had to speak quickly while it made sense in my head. "We've wasted so much time already. We've missed so much together. I know with one hundred percent certainty how I feel and if you do, too, then let's do this. Together. Finally."

"This?"

"You and me." I grabbed her hands. "The way it always should have been."

"Are you asking me to marry you?" There was a teasing tone in her voice, and her eyes sparkled with mischief, but I didn't laugh.

"I will," I told her confidently. "You can count on that. But for now, move in with me. Be with me. The way we always should have been together."

She didn't say no, but I saw the questions in her eyes. The laughter died on her lips, and the sparkle of her eyes turned cloudy. "My job...I—"

"Will only ever set foot in that club again if you *want* to. Not because you *have* to. I'm sure your resignation was heard loud and clear last night."

Her eyes widened, and she dropped her head a little. "I need that job," she said. "I'm going to school." Her voice was hesitant, but there was no mistaking the thread of strength and determination I loved so much there, too.

"Of course. I support that completely. You never should have quit before you finished your degree. And I support whatever you want to do. Always." I blinked, remembering what initially led us to this moment. "Except for stealing money for tuition. I will not support that." I pinned her with my gaze. "Which reminds me, we still need to discuss an appropriate punishment for that."

I didn't miss the flare of her nostrils, the darkening of her pupils, or the flush on her bare chest. *Damn.* But one thing at a time. I forced myself to concentrate on the issue at hand.

"No more stealing," I said again.

"I only did it—"

"I know why you did it." I interrupted her. "I'll take care of the tuition. *All* of it."

"No." She shook her head and tried to pull away but I held her fast. "I can't let you do that, Phillip."

I pulled her closer to me on the bed so I could have one hand on her thigh and one cupping her cheek. "You can," I said firmly. "And you will, because that's what people who love each other do for each other. And I love you. So let me do this, Abigail. Let me do all of it. Everything. All for you."

"I don't need you to do everything for me."

It was my turn to laugh. "Truer words have never been spoken." I squeezed her thigh gently. "You're strong and independent, and you don't *need* anything from me. I love that about you. And I'm not asking you to give up any part of what makes you who you are. I'd never do that. Especially after everything you've been through. But I am asking you to be my partner. Know that you *can* do it alone, but choose not to. Choose me. Because I choose you." I tipped her chin up with one finger so she was looking me directly in the eyes. "I love you, Abigail. I always have and I always will. Forever."

She swallowed, and a soft smile crossed her lips. "I love you, too," she said after a moment. "More than I ever knew." She closed her eyes as I kissed her tenderly.

When we parted and Abigail once more opened her eyes, I could see it on her face. She'd made up her mind.

Chapter Twelve

"SO YOU'RE JUST MOVING?" Darla held up the empty duffel bag I'd thrown on my bed, later that day. "Just like that? No discussion? No time to think? Just...moving?"

I knew my friends would have questions. Hell, I had questions. It hadn't even been a full week since that day in the pro shop when I'd taken those bills from Phillip's money clip and stuffed them in my bra, and here I was, packing up all my things and moving out of my shitty little apartment into his mansion.

It was all happening ridiculously fast.

I never made decisions so quickly. And I almost never made a life-altering decision without at the very least consulting my friends.

But this was different.

Sure, it might be crazy and reckless and a disaster waiting to happen.

But it wasn't.

I felt that in my bones.

I'd never been so sure about anything in my life.

"Hey," I said. "You're the one who told me to go out and

have a little fun." I shot Darla a look over my shoulder. "We only live once, right?"

"I was talking about having wild sex with a hot man," Darla said with a shake of her blonde head. "Not uprooting your entire life and moving in with the hot man. That is entirely different." She gave me a pointed look, but thankfully she turned and started stuffing T-shirts into the duffel bag with another small shake of her head, this time to herself. She knew me well enough to know that she couldn't talk me out of something once I'd made up my mind. "The sex must have been pretty damn good." She muttered it under her breath, but I'd heard it.

"Oh, no," I said as seriously as I could.

Just as I knew she would, Darla spun around, T-shirt still in her hand. "What? Please don't tell me you're moving in with a man and the sex isn't even good." She threw her head back dramatically. "I couldn't bear it."

I couldn't help it; I chuckled a little bit under my breath. I couldn't have kept the grin off my face if I'd tried. My body still tingled from the memories of every toe-curling, body-stiffening orgasm Phillip had given me. And there had definitely been more than a few. In less than twenty-four hours, I'd had better sex than I'd had in my whole life combined.

"It's not just good," I finally said. "It's freaking amazing! I mean…toe-curling, want to do it all the time, best sex I've ever had."

Darla squealed and clapped her hands. "I knew it! I knew it!" She climbed over the bed and gave me a tight hug.

It took me a few moments to realize Jessie hadn't joined in the excitement. I pulled away from Darla and looked to my other friend.

Jessie stood next to the closet with a frown on her face. "This is a pretty big decision, Abby," she said. "I mean, you haven't been on your own for very long yet. Maybe you might want to just date for a while and see how you feel?"

"I appreciate your concern, Jessie. I really do." I couldn't stop the smile from crossing my face. "But I know exactly how I feel. I am totally and completely in love. I've only ever felt like this once before."

"With Phillip?" Jessie asked slowly.

I nodded. "With Phillip."

"I believe you." A smile spread across my friend's face as well. "And I couldn't be happier for you. And honestly, maybe a little jealous, too."

I gave Jessie a hug. If it could happen for me, it could happen for her, and I told her so before turning back to our tasks.

Phillip had tried to convince me to let movers come and handle my tiny apartment, but it was important that I do it myself. After all, I'd just made a big deal about being independent and strong. Besides, it gave me a chance to catch up with the girls and help them understand why I was moving so quickly. Not that it *was* quick. Not really. After all, we'd loved each other for over fifteen years. Even if it took us a long time to figure it out and come to it, now that we had, we didn't want to wait anymore.

My friends were supportive, the way I knew they would be. But I would have been surprised if they didn't have a few questions, as well as a few concerns. After all, it was all sort of coming out of nowhere, and to say it was a massive change would be an understatement.

"So the sex..." I turned to see Jessie holding a sweater she'd been folding, watching me. "It's..."

It surprised me that it was Jessie who was the one that asked about the sex first. But something about the way her eyes sparkled told me maybe my friend was finally getting ready to have a little bit of excitement in her own life, so I obliged by telling her every single detail.

"Against the wall?" Her mouth fell open. "Like, right in the foyer of the house? Doesn't he have a live-in housekeeper? She could have—"

"The risk of getting caught is all part of the fun, right?"

We both turned to see Britt in the doorway. "Sorry I'm late," she said as I lifted my eyebrow in a question, but she simply shrugged. "What? Just because I don't make much time for it, doesn't mean I don't actually have any sex."

I laughed.

"And I've definitely had my share of up against the wall sex," Britt added before turning to Jessie. "I take it you haven't?"

Our friend bit her bottom lip and shook her head, and I instantly felt badly for her. I may not have had a very exciting sex life when I was married to Daniel, at least not compared to what I was experiencing with Phillip, but it was still pretty good. I couldn't ever say I was unsatisfied.

I knew the same wasn't true for Jessie. She'd been the first of us to get married, almost straight out of high school, with the first serious boyfriend she'd ever had and as far as I knew, she'd only ever had sex with him.

It's not that Barrett was a bad guy. He was just...boring and kind of dull.

Okay, he was very dull. And it turned out that he was also not a great husband. Shortly after their wedding, when young and broke, they discovered they were pregnant with twins, Jessie had risen to the challenge and made sure that even though they were far from ready to be parents that her kids never lacked for anything. Barrett, on the other hand, more or less checked out. From the outside looking in, Jessie had everything under control. Two great kids, a husband who provided, and for all intents and purposes, a great life.

It wasn't until after their divorce that we all learned the truth. Their marriage had been dead almost since it began, and Jessie had been deeply unhappy for almost all of it. Seeing that pain in my friend had hurt deeply, especially because I had no idea she'd been suffering. In the years since, Jessie opened up more and more about how things had been, including the complete and total lack of a sex life they'd had.

But now…maybe that could change.

I sat next to my friend on the bed and took the sweater from her. "You should," I said. "Have sex up against a wall, I mean." I glanced over at Darla, whose grin split her face.

"One hundred percent you should," she said. "And on a table, in the shower, outside, and—"

"Wait." Jessie interrupted her. "Outside?"

She looked around the room at all of us in turn. We all nodded in agreement. Sandy was still in the kitchen, packing up, but that was probably a good thing. Because, as far as I knew, as much as she'd loved her husband, I don't remember her ever talking about their sex life much, which I was pretty sure meant it was fairly tame and likely didn't include anything out of the bedroom, let alone outdoors.

Jessie shook her head slowly and laughed. "Wow," she said. "I mean, I knew I was missing out, but I had no idea." She threw her head back and groaned. "Okay," she admitted. "You're right. I'm *way* overdue for a little of that kind of fun."

"Yeah you are!" Darla shouted her encouragement from the dresser.

"Kitchen's all packed for donation," Sandy said as she appeared in the doorway. "What's Jessie overdue for?"

"Hot sex!" Darla and I shouted at the same time before breaking out into giggles, just as we would have twenty years earlier. "Seriously," I said when I recovered. "It will change your life. Literally."

"Clearly." Britt nodded pointedly to the stack of boxes. "But not everyone can be as lucky as you, Abby. Aspen Valley is still a pretty small town. There are only so many men to go around."

"It's not that small," I protested. "And why can't you all be as lucky as me? There's no rule that says that." I tucked a few more things in a box and looked up as an idea popped into my head. "In fact," I said slowly, until all eyes were on me. "I think we should make a pact."

"A pact?" Sandy raised an eyebrow. "Like when we were kids?"

"Exactly." The ladies drew closer until we were all sitting on my old single bed. The idea wasn't fully formulated. But listening to Jessie and seeing just how much she was missing out on—never mind Sandy and Britt, too...Darla, I wasn't worried about, not as far as good sex went. But, maybe she could bene-fit, too. The idea was coming to me quickly, so I blurted it out.

"I don't know if I would have been able to work up the courage to go ahead with everything with Phillip if it hadn't been for you all convincing me to just go for it."

"So really, you have us to thank for all this?" Britt laughed but I nodded seriously.

"Yes." I looked around at my girlfriends. We'd been in one another's lives for so long, we knew one another almost as well as we knew ourselves, maybe even better some days. "And you know what, I think we could all use a little bit of a push toward something else." I was met with looks of confusion so I contin-ued. "Britt, you work too hard."

She opened her mouth to protest, but closed it again because she knew it was true.

"Maybe a push toward some sexy good times of your own

might help you loosen up a little?" She shrugged in response, but didn't say no, so I moved on to Jessie. "And you, Jessie, between your kids and the diner, you've never given yourself the opportunity to let loose a little bit."

"Or a lot," she said. "You're not wrong."

I turned slowly to Sandy. It had been years since her husband passed away, but we all knew how much she'd loved him. "Sandy? You don't really think that Greg would want you to live like a nun forever, do you?"

We all waited and watched for her response.

After a moment, she nodded slowly. "He wouldn't. He told me as much. In fact, he'd be pretty pissed with me if he knew I had."

I didn't expect that. I smiled softly and moved to Darla, who shrugged. "I don't need a push."

But didn't she?

I decided to wait to push my point with Darla.

"Okay," Jessie said. "So we all need a little push. But what does that have to do with a pact?"

"Right." Britt nodded at Jessie and looked at me. "What are you proposing?" She crossed her legs and leaned in, curious. "That we all encourage each other to just *go for it?*"

"Yes," I said. That was the idea in a nutshell. It really was that simple. "Instead of taking the safe and boring route, the next time one of us has the opportunity to step out of her comfort zone, even a little bit, they send a text and…we all support and encourage her to just go for it. No matter what. Life is too short not to take a chance. Even if it's risky."

"It has to be safe," Sandy added.

"Obviously." I nodded. "But we're all big girls, and we're not stupid. We won't do anything dangerous and as long as we're letting each other know…"

"It'll be fine," Britt finished. "And it could be fun." She nodded. "I'm in."

Darla laughed. "Well, I already do this pretty much every day, so I'll be the lead cheerleader. I'm in."

"You're not wrong," Jessie agreed with a groan. "The twins are almost grown and gone. I need something to occupy my time besides *Rosie's*. And I could really use some hot, up against the wall sex of my own." She grinned. "Why not? I'm in."

All eyes turned to Sandy. I still wasn't convinced she would agree. She was way too straight laced and conservative. But then, much to my surprise, a small smile played across her lips.

"Okay," she said. "I'm in."

We all laughed and collapsed into a group hug on the bed.

"Okay." Jessie pulled away after a moment. "So if we're really doing this, how do we know when one of us has the opportunity to *go for it?*" She held up her fingers in air quotes.

"Good point." Britt sat up. "We need a code word. Something that signifies to the others that we need a push."

Darla grinned wickedly. "Almost like a dare that you can't say no to."

"Exactly." Sandy nodded.

"Let's just keep it simple," I suggested. "Maybe just ask the others if you should *go for it.*"

"Right!" Sandy smiled, surprising me yet again. "And the rest of us *have* to say yes."

"Okay, but…" Britt held up her hand. "We need an escape plan, too."

We all turned to her in question.

She pulled her shoulders back. "Look," Britt said. "I agree this is a good plan. I mean, we could all use a little push from our comfort zones. But if there's ever a situation that has a red flag, we vote."

"Vote?"

ELENA AITKEN

"We vote." She addressed me. "For example, if I thought this whole thing with Phillip seemed dangerous, I'd call a vote. Majority rules."

I shrugged. It wasn't a bad idea and we all agreed, because why wouldn't we? We'd been friends most of our lives. There was no other group of women I'd trust my life to, and I knew they all felt the same way.

Besides, who said your forties were too late to take a risk and have a little fun? Or some fabulous sex? We might all be a little late to the party, but *finally* it was our turn to have some of the fun we'd always deserved.

It had only been three hours since the car had dropped Abigail at her apartment. Of course I'd agreed to letting her pack up her things with her friends, but there was no way I could allow her to drive away in that deathtrap of a rust bucket she called a car. As soon as she was settled, I would take her to pick out the car of her choice. Something just as sexy as she was. Maybe a stick shift with some real power behind it.

I swallowed down the thought before I let it take hold. As it was, I'd been in an almost constant state of arousal for the last few days and now that I'd finally had Abigail in my bed, I didn't see that changing anytime soon.

"Phillip. Sorry I'm late."

Trent Thomas joined me at the highly polished bar where I'd been nursing a whiskey while I waited for him. His invite for a drink had been perfect timing. Anything to keep my mind off Abigail and exactly what I was going to do to her in *our* bed when I finally got her home for good.

"No problem." I gestured to the stool next to me. "I'm glad we could make this work. Something has come up, and I think

I'll be taking a bit of time off, maybe get away for a bit." It was an idea I hadn't discussed with Abigail yet, but I was hoping she'd be just as excited to take a little holiday as I was. It didn't even matter where we went, as long as it was together.

"Sounds good." Trent ordered a whiskey for himself and turned to me. "I'll be here when you get back. The opportunities are better out here than I originally anticipated."

I lifted my drink in agreement as he accepted his from the bartender. We clinked glasses and each drank deeply. "We'll have to catch up when I get back."

"Absolutely." Trent put his glass down. "No rush. I have plenty to keep me busy. And I'm looking forward to getting to know Aspen Valley a little better. I've only been here for a few days, but I have to tell you, it seems a whole lot more exciting than I expected."

I couldn't help but laugh. "I assume you're referring to the club the other night?"

"I most certainly am."

I'd forgotten that Trent was there. Not that I gave a shit. I didn't care one bit who'd borne witness to what happened between Abigail and me that night.

"It looked pretty intense," Trent said. "The two of you are…"

"Going to live happily ever after." *Very* happily ever after, if the last few days had been any indication. I couldn't get enough of that woman. She was like a drug, and I continually needed another fix.

My old friend snorted.

"I take it you're single?"

"Very," he said wryly. "Never met a woman who could hold my interest longer than a few fucks." He shrugged and drank from his glass.

Before I could respond, my phone chirped with an

incoming text message. *Abigail.* She was done packing and ready for me to pick her up. My cock twitched in anticipation of seeing her soon. I raised my almost-empty glass. "You never know, Trent. Aspen Valley might just change all that. There are some pretty fantastic women here." I tossed the rest of the whiskey into my mouth before dropping a few bills on the counter and setting the glass on top. "Drinks on me. Sorry I can't stay."

Trent grinned wickedly. "She must be something to have you jumping up like that."

"No." I shook my head once. "She's not something, Trent." I pushed up from the bar and looked my old friend in the eye. "She's *everything.*"

Chapter Thirteen

A FEW HOURS LATER, the few possessions I had were boxed up and ready for the movers to gather up and bring to Phillip's mansion. Everything else, which admittedly wasn't much, was to be donated. I'd officially quit my job at the Aspen Valley Country Club, not that anyone was surprised after Phillip and I had very publicly introduced our relationship to the world—and ourselves—at the party the night before.

And I was finally *home*, cuddled up, quite happily in Phillip's arms on the couch in the living room with two half-filled wine glasses on the table in front of us.

"Things have a funny way of working out, don't they?" I nestled in closer and his arm squeezed me tight. "I mean, if I hadn't have taken that money, we wouldn't be here right now."

He chuckled. "You mean, if I hadn't have stopped into the pro shop that day. You don't really think that was an accident, do you?"

I sat up a little. "You mean, you came in to talk to me? I thought you forgot to return the jacket." I narrowed my eyes in question.

Phillip only shrugged casually in response. "Maybe I forgot to return the jacket on purpose?"

"Did you?"

"Does it matter?"

It didn't. But only because my poor decision in taking his money had led to the opportunity for us to reconnect. I said as much.

"Okay," he said with a grin. "If you want to play this game…" He pulled away and shifted on the couch so we faced each other. "But if I hadn't made you a deal you couldn't have refused…"

"What if I had?" The question had just occurred to me. "I mean, would you really have turned me in?"

He didn't hesitate with his answer. "Never."

"So why make me a deal? And…kind of a ballsy one at that." I crossed my arms and gave him a playful smile. It had been a risky offer, almost offensive, really. Not that I would have seen it that way. Not coming from Phillip.

He wiggled his eyebrow and smirked in that oh so cocky way he had that made my body pulse with desire. "Because I knew you'd say yes."

Oh yes. He was cocky.

"And if I didn't?"

"You did." He moved up the couch almost like a cat, so he was moving on top of me, pressing me back into the cushions. "And I knew you would," he said when he was directly over top of me. "Because you, my love, are stubborn, smart, feisty, and sexy as hell."

I laughed a little, and he caught my bottom lip gently between his teeth and tugged. Heat flared through me as he kissed me hard.

"And you can't say no to me," he growled against my lips.

"Oh yeah? You don't think so?" I pulled back a little.

"I know so."

So. Very. Cocky.

"What if I told you no, now?" I was playing with him, and he knew it. Because he was right. I couldn't say no to him. Just the same way I knew he couldn't say no to me. The same spell he had on me, I had on him.

Phillip sat back so he was still overtop me, but could slide his hands down my sides to my leather belt. His fingers traced the edge of the belt, teasing the bare skin under my T-shirt as he moved. With one hand on the buckle, he used his other hand to slip between my legs. I moaned at his touch; even through the denim, my body responded, heat and moisture instantly flooding to my core. I wriggled my hips a little against his hand.

"You want to say no?"

I bit my bottom lip but didn't answer.

"Abigail?" He pressed his hand firmer between my legs.

I shook my head. "No."

He froze. "You're saying no?"

Oh, he was playing now.

"I'm saying no, I don't want to say no."

His grin was wicked as he worked to undo my buckle and slide the leather free. "That's what I thought."

I lifted my hips as Phillip stood and pulled my jeans and panties down and tossed them to the side, leaving me bare on the couch.

He licked his lips a little, which only sent another shot of heat through me. Phillip bent to kiss me. I closed my eyes, waiting to receive his mouth on mine. Instead, he dropped to his knees, put his hands on my thighs, and pulled them apart, exposing me to him completely. My eyes flew open in time to see his head dip down between my thighs. Before I could say anything, his tongue licked my already wet seam and I cried out.

Reflexively, I wiggled, but his hands held me by the hips, unable to move as his tongue licked, swirled, and dipped inside me. Just when I thought I couldn't take much more, he sucked my clit into his mouth, and I completely shattered, coming apart in a hot, hard orgasm. Phillip didn't release his grip on me until the last shudder ran through my body.

"Damn, that was hot." He stood in front of me, and casually wiped his face as he stripped himself of his own clothes. "But I'm not done with you yet, my love."

I was totally spent, but when he flicked his lips up in a devilish grin and extended his hand to me, I couldn't resist. My body responded with another impossible wave of desire.

I stood in front of him as he lifted my shirt off and over my head, and then he kissed me hard, pressing his lips on mine so I could taste myself on him. Heat and moisture once more pooled between my legs, and I moaned into his kiss.

The kiss ended abruptly and Phillip spun me until my back was pressed up against him. He palmed each of my breasts in his hands and squeezed as he kissed my neck. "You are so fucking gorgeous."

His hard, throbbing cock pressed up against me, and I ground myself back into it, pushing him further to the edge I knew he must be getting close to.

As I expected, he let out a low moan of his own, but then, with two quick steps, he walked me forward to the couch. With a firm pressure on my low back, he guided me down and over the arm of the other stuffed sofa.

He ran his hands down over my bare skin, digging his fingers into the soft flesh of my ass. "Abigail, you are too much." His voice was rough, barely contained. A moment later, I felt him hard and hot against my entrance. "I will never get enough."

I arched my back; Phillip gripped my hips hard and pulled me to him as he pushed into me. I groaned with the fullness of him, and he gave me a moment to grow used to him, but only a moment before he moved urgently within me. With one hand gripped on my hip, he pulled me hard against him, before pushing me forward into the couch. It was both rough and tender as his free hand found my breast, alternately squeezing and caressing as together we crested into powerful orgasms.

We didn't bother getting dressed again. I curled into Phillip on the couch, enjoying the feel of his hot skin against mine. He pulled an oversized fluffy blanket over us and handed me my glass of wine.

"I guess you were right," I said after I took a sip.

"About?"

"Not being able to say no to you."

He chuckled. "I love it." He pressed a kiss to the top of my head. "And I love you."

I turned so I looked up to him. "And I love you."

"I will never get tired of hearing those words." His smile lit up his face.

"Good. Because I will never get tired of saying them."

We sat in silence for a moment, each enjoying our wine and the delicious satisfaction that only comes from amazing sex.

"Can I tell you something, Phillip?"

He smoothed my hair with his hand. "Anything. Always."

"In a way, I'm glad we didn't end up together back then." I felt him stiffen next to me, but he didn't protest. "I know it sounds stupid, but...do you think it would have been so perfect if it had worked out back then?"

He was quiet for a moment as he mulled over what I'd said.

Finally, I heard him exhale slowly. I twisted in his arms so I could see his face when he spoke.

"I can't agree to that, Abigail." He shook his head slowly. "Because that would be admitting that I was okay without. And I wasn't." He looked me in the eye and brushed a stray hair from my forehead. "Every day I was apart from you, something was missing." His lips slowly twitched into a smile. "But I'm not one to look back—what's the point?"

The arm he had wrapped around me slid down my side and pulled me up onto his lap. I curled into his embrace. I was safe. I was loved. And happier than I'd ever been.

"Because now," Phillip continued, "all is right with the world. You're here. You're with me, and finally, you're mine."

"Finally yours," I said, trying the words out as I looked into his eyes. He tilted my chin up and kissed me deeply until any thoughts of what could have been were replaced with what *was*. Because Phillip was right: nothing else mattered.

He was mine. And I was his.

Finally.

Epilogue

"YOU HAVE to let us throw you a party." Darla lifted her glass of whiskey to her mouth but lowered it again before taking a sip. "I mean, it's your birthday, Abby."

"I agree." Jessie, who'd been continually cleaning the diner since we'd arrived for our weekly drinks and catch-up session, finally sat down across from me. "We need a party."

"We do not need a party." I sipped at my martini. It wasn't that I was against celebrating my birthday. Not at all. It's just that it had been a strange year—to say the least—and I just wanted something a little more low-key than a party.

In fact, staying in with Phillip and a bottle of wine sounded pretty perfect to me. Especially if I put on one of the sexy lingerie pieces he continually brought home for me.

It had only been three weeks since I'd moved in with him, but he hadn't wasted any time spoiling me rotten. Not that I was naive enough to think the lingerie was *all* about me. In fact, judging from his reaction the night before, I was pretty sure that the black leather corset with the garters and stockings was just as much for him as it had been for me.

Maybe more.

I didn't bother hiding the wicked smile as I remembered the way he'd bent me over the couch and fucked me hard from behind.

Oh yes, it had been a *very* good night.

"Hello." Sandy waved a hand in front of my face. "Where did you go? We were talking and—"

"Judging by that blush on her cheeks," Britt said, "I'd guess she was thinking about that sexy man of hers and something very dirty and probably scandalous that they've been doing together."

I wiggled my eyebrows because she was not wrong.

"Not that you'd know." Darla laughed at Britt. "When was the last time you got laid?"

"Hey." Britt pointed a finger at her friend and for a moment, I thought she might actually get upset with Darla for...well, being Darla. Instead, she shrugged and dropped her hand. "It's true. It's been so long, I don't even know if anything works down there anymore."

"Oh, I assure you it works," I teased. "You just need a little practice. In fact..." I looked around at my girlfriends. "I thought we had a pact. Don't tell me that none of you haven't even had the opportunity to live a little? I thought we agreed."

There were a series of murmurs and shrugs, but finally, Jessie spoke. "It's not that I'm avoiding it," she said. "I mean..." She dropped her head back for a minute before looking up again. "Believe me when I say that I am *more* than ready for a little fun. I swear I am. It's just..."

"What?" Sandy leaned on her elbows. "It's just what?"

"Honestly?"

We all nodded.

"How am I supposed to have any kind of adventure when I spend all of my time here?" Jessie waved her arms around the empty diner. "And if I'm not here, I'm home, making sure the kids are packing and ready to go. Can you believe they're both leaving me for college in less than a week?" She wiped at her eyes, and Britt wrapped an arm around her to give her a quick squeeze.

"You're going to be okay," Darla said. "I promise."

"Besides," I said. "Once they're finally moved and settled next week, think of all the extra time you're going to have. Your time is coming, Jessie. I can feel it."

She nodded and lifted her wine to her mouth for a deep drink. "I hope so. I really do," she said when she lowered the glass. "Because I mean it when I say that I'm more than ready. I really am."

"I believe you." I did believe her. Jessie had been alone for *way* too long, and no one worked harder than she did. Except for maybe Britt. But that was a different kind of hard work. And as far as I was concerned, they were both equally overdue for some sexy fun and adventure. I couldn't even begin to explain to them how amazing my life was since I took a chance on Phillip. Although, I certainly tried.

"I think we're all missing the point here," Sandy said. "We were talking about the birthday party that Abby needs to have."

I groaned and dropped my head to the table. "Will it make you feel better if I tell you that I'm almost one hundred percent sure that Phillip has a surprise planned for me?"

"A little." Darla shrugged.

"He better," Britt said.

"Of course he does." Jessie winked across the table at me. "And no doubt it's going to be exactly what you want, Abby. That's all that really matters. Isn't it, ladies?"

"No way," Darla said. "I want a party." Jessie shot her a look and Darla quickly shook her head. "Fine," she said. "Whatever Abby wants."

I laughed and blew her a kiss because I really did have the best friends.

#

It was Abigail's birthday and I had the perfect surprise planned.

I'd racked my brain coming up with exactly the right thing for my love.

I knew she didn't want a party.

A trip? Of course. But her classes were starting soon and she was committed to her education. A fact I was very proud of her for. She worked hard.

Which meant she needed to play hard.

And a little release of a sexual nature sounded like a pretty good plan.

So the plan had come together, and I could hardly wait to see what her reaction was.

Having Abigail back in my life in such a perfect way was literally the best thing in the world. I had never been happier. Or more sexually satisfied. It was true what they said: good things were definitely worth the wait.

If it meant having Abigail in my life every day and in my bed every night, I would do it all over again. Lucky for me, I didn't have to wait. Not anymore. She was mine. And I intended to keep it that way.

I also intended to keep things fun and exciting. Which was why this birthday surprise was going to be amazing.

According to my watch, it was almost time. Of course I'd been ready for ages, dressed in my signature black suit, with matte black shirt. I left my office behind and waited for my love in the foyer.

I'd arranged for her to be pampered for the majority of the day. I'd brought in a masseuse, a hair stylist, makeup artist, and a handful of spa technicians for body wraps, a pedicure, manicure, and whatever else they saw fit to do. She deserved to be pampered and spoiled.

And teased.

The thought made my cock harden in my pants. I adjusted myself and took a breath, forcing myself to stay in control. She liked it when I was in control, and for this evening to play out the way I had planned for her, I needed my control firmly in place.

When Abigail appeared at the top of the stairs in the black dress I'd picked out for her, she literally took my breath away. The fabric of the dress shimmered as it hugged her body. It dipped scandalously low between her breasts, and I knew the back of the dress dipped even lower, leaving her back almost completely exposed. There were two very high slits on either side of the dress, so her lean, sculpted legs would peek out as she walked. Abigail had a gorgeous body. It deserved to be showcased. It was a risqué dress, but it was also equally classy and Abigail was stunning.

Slowly, she made her way down the curved staircase in impossibly high heels that I had also picked out for her. Just as I knew they would, her legs looked amazing on display with the heels, lengthening them.

Damn. My cock throbbed, but I willed myself, again, to stay in control.

"Happy birthday, darling." I took her hand and kissed it. "You look absolutely..." I shook my head a little, taking my time with the compliment. "Outstanding."

"Thank you." She beamed, her face lighting up with the smile. I loved how she accepted a compliment instead of shying away. It was sexy as hell. "This dress is...it's actually pretty incredible." Abigail spun a little. "I don't think I've ever worn anything like it."

I was positive she'd never worn anything like it. I slid a

hand along her back and around her waist to the high slit of her dress. "Did you have a nice day?"

"So nice." She closed her eyes for a moment. "I feel completely relaxed and almost kind of lazy."

Lazy? I'd fix that.

I pushed the thin fabric aside and slipped my hand along the top of her thigh until my fingers brushed along the lips of her bare pussy.

Her eyes popped open, but she didn't pull away. "There were no panties laid out with the dress."

I shook my head. "This dress doesn't really lend itself to panties." Brazen, which was what the evening called for, I stepped closer and slipped my finger between her legs and inside her wet heat.

She groaned, her lips parted slightly, but she didn't take her eyes off me.

"Do you trust me?"

Abigail didn't hesitate. "Completely."

"Good." I moved closer, so our lips were inches apart. "Because I wanted to get you something special for your birthday." I wiggled my finger and she groaned again; her legs buckled a little. "Trust and control."

Her eyes opened wide in question, the way I knew they would. Abigail was a strong, independent woman. It would be a complicated concept for her to wrap her mind around; I knew this. I also knew how much she'd enjoy her present as soon as she accepted it.

"If you trust me and release control," I explained as I moved my finger, still inside her, slowly and precisely, "you'll understand completely."

#

Trust and control?

I had no idea what he was talking about, but with the way

his finger moved, I didn't care. The need he built inside me so effortlessly clouded my brain. Besides, I did trust Phillip. With my life. And it was my birthday...

He'd already pampered me. I'd been rubbed and scrubbed, waxed and lotioned. I'd put on the most gorgeous, scandalous dress I'd ever seen in my life, and now I stood, fully dressed, in the foyer of his house with his finger inside me, only moments away from climaxing all over his hand.

Yes.

I trusted him.

I nodded.

"Do you promise?" He crooked his finger, causing me to gasp. "You'll trust me and let me be in control?"

Fuck yes. I would agree to anything if it meant he'd finish.

"I promise." I managed the words before I bit my bottom lip, ready for the release that was sure to come next.

Instead, he withdrew his finger, and took my hand in his. "Good," was all he said as he led me to the door. "You're going to have a very special birthday."

Outside, a long, black limousine waited in the drive.

"Where are we going?" I tried to peek out the window as we drove, but I couldn't see much through the blacked-out windows, not that it mattered. "Not the club?"

"Control, remember?"

I tilted my head and gave him a look.

Phillip knew how hard it was for me to relinquish control of any kind. "You promised," he reminded me.

I had to bite back my response about how I was under the expectation that I was about to get an orgasm, but instead, I just nodded. *I had promised, after all.*

"Don't worry," Phillip said. "You'll enjoy it." I sat back against the seat and Phillip reached forward to pick up jewelry box. "First," he said. "A gift."

I shook my head. "You've given me enough. I can't accept this." No doubt it was a flashy necklace with diamonds and other gemstones and something ridiculously expensive that I couldn't possibly accept. I didn't want him to think that he had to shower me in gifts. That's not what this was about. Being with him was my gift. The way he made me feel after way too long not being loved—emotionally *or* physically—the way I deserved was gift enough.

"Open it."

It was a command. And it was sexy as hell.

I did as I was told and lifted the lid, expecting a glitzy necklace.

But that's not at all what was inside.

"What is it?" I lifted the delicate chains from the box. It looked almost like a necklace, but there were too many chains. A triangle piece made up of jewels and chains so delicate, it almost looked like fabric, was suspended in the middle.

"It's a toy." The edge in his voice gave him away, and I turned to stare at him.

"What kind of toy?"

His grin was wicked and my nipples hardened in anticipation.

Trust and control.

"Put it on." Phillip lifted the thin fabric of my dress to the side, exposing me completely. "Just slip it up over your legs and slide it over your hips."

I understood at once what I was holding and, with a sly grin, did as I was told. I bent down and put one leg and then the other through the thin chains and shimmied them up to my hips. The mesh jeweled triangle settled between my legs and the weight of it felt good. Sexy.

"Perfect." Phillip admired his gift before smoothing the fabric of my dress back into place.

"Are you going to tell me how it works?"

He grinned again. *Damn but he was sexy.* I liked this take-control side of him. It was fun and the anticipation of what was to come started to excite me. A lot.

Phillip cupped my cheek and kissed me gently. Almost chastely. "It's about trust," he said simply. "And part of that is trusting me to take care of your pleasure, my love." He ran one finger from my lips, down one breast and up to the other. "Are you hungry?"

I was. But not for food. I wanted him with a ferocity that surprised me. I nodded and worked hard to control my breathing.

Hungry didn't even begin to explain how he made me feel.

\#

I knew the suspense was killing her. It didn't come naturally to Abigail to give up control, and the very fact that she was trusting me in this way was huge. And I wasn't going to let her down.

In the meantime, I knew it was making her crazy that she hadn't quite figured out what was going on yet.

I could tell her.

But I waited.

We got out of the car and walked inside, where I saw her reaction to the five-star restaurant in the city where I'd made a primo reservation for the best table. It had only taken one call, and I'd skipped the three-month waiting list. Knowing that I could do what I wanted, when I wanted, had always been a turn-on for me. But the power of wealth was nothing compared to the need that had flared through me when I saw her slip my present over her hips and settle it into place over her clit—that I knew without even checking would already be throbbing in need. I'd had to look away.

A man could only take so much.

The real question was how much would Abigail be able to take.

I ordered a bottle of wine and still I waited.

We took our time looking over the menus and choosing our entrees. I didn't miss the way she squirmed in her seat. No doubt from the anticipation.

I drew it out further by making small talk. Asking her about her classes and which ones she was most excited to start.

After a few minutes, she seemed to forget herself and the promise she'd made me. "Are you ever going to tell me—"

I held up a finger and she immediately swallowed the rest of the question. "Don't forget your promise." Chastised, she looked down for a moment, and I doubled down. "I think you owe me an apology."

Her head popped up. Her mouth made an O of protest, and a red-hot blush pinked her skin and traveled down between her breasts. I longed to push the fabric of her dress aside and pinch each of her nipples in turn, the way I knew would make her cry out in pleasure. Instead, I grinned wickedly and finally she swallowed hard.

"I'm sorry, Philip. I remember my promise."

Damn. My cock stiffened almost to the point of pain sitting across from her.

I took a sip of wine to pull myself together. I would not rush things. I slipped my hand in my pocket and wrapped my fingers around the small remote I had there.

The waiter appeared a moment after, with our entrees. I waited patiently while she cut a small piece of her duck and placed it in her mouth.

"This is delicious! I've never tasted anything so good."

I nodded and took a bite of my own meal.

Abigail cut another piece and moments before it touched

her lips, I made my move. With my fingers still on the remote in my pocket, I pushed the top button.

"Oh!" She dropped her fork to her plate with a clatter, and I pushed the button again, cutting off the vibration I'd just sent directly to her clit. "What was—"

"Don't forget we're in a very public place, Abigail."

Her eyes opened wide as she realized exactly what was happening. She opened her mouth—no doubt to protest. But, obviously remembering her promise, she closed it again and gave me a sly look.

I took a sip of wine and waited until she followed suit before I pushed the button again. She swallowed hard, and put both hands flat on the table, her eyes wide with wonder.

This time, I left it on. Her breath came fast, her breasts rising and falling. I knew the setting was set to low. The vibrations and weight of the jewel on her clit would soon drive her crazy. And as soon as I knew she was on the edge and dripping with need was when I'd take her home and let her lose complete control.

I carried on the conversation normally, proceeding with my meal. After a few moments, Abigail did as well, but I could see her shift in her seat in an effort to relieve the growing pressure on her clit. After a few minutes had passed, she set down her fork, abandoning her meal altogether.

I switched off the vibration and took a slow sip of my wine. "Not hungry, Abigail?"

She shook her head slowly. Watching her try to keep herself under control was one of the sexiest things I've ever witnessed. She reached for her wine and took a sip as she relaxed without the constant stimulation. I eased her back into easy conversation, and she even took another bite or two of her dinner. Good. It was expensive.

"Are you enjoying your meal?"

"I am," she said with a slight smile. "The duck is some of the—"

With her caught off guard, I took the opportunity to increase the vibration level and pressed the button on the remote.

"Oh my—" She caught herself and sucked her bottom lip into her mouth, but not before she'd caught the attention of some nearby diners.

"She's really enjoying her meal," I said innocently. "I recommend the duck."

I left the vibration on again, this time at a higher intensity that I knew would have her on the edge of coming apart right there at the table with everyone watching. The idea that she was only barely controlling herself was insanely sexy.

I reminded her again that we were in public. And when she looked up at me with hunger in her eyes that even the most expensive meal would be unable to satisfy, it was time to go.

I threw a stack of cash on the table and stood, waiting for her to join me. I could have turned off the vibration long enough to walk to the car, but it was way too enticing watching her trying to pretend as if everything were normal when really every step she took brought her closer to coming right there in the restaurant in front of everyone.

I told her it would be a birthday surprise she would remember. And I wasn't finished yet.

\#

Every part of me vibrated with need. I couldn't remember ever being in such a constant state of arousal since…well, ever. There was no way I ever could have done this with anyone else. But with Philip, I'd meant it when I said I trusted him completely. The idea that the other diners might have known I was on the verge of an orgasm while they enjoyed their expensive meals, it was…well…exciting.

The moment the driver opened the door, I practically dove for the cover of the car and Phillip slipped in behind me.

"Did you enjoy your dinner?" His grin was wicked as he slipped a hand over my thigh. He still hadn't shut off that blasted toy and with the weight of his hand so close to my clit, it only increased the pressure low in my belly.

"You know damn well I barely ate a thing."

"So, did you enjoy it?"

I licked my lips and nodded. "Very much."

"Good." He chuckled, but I wasn't in the laughing mood. There was only one thing I needed.

"My turn," I said. "Take your pants off."

I thought for a minute he might say no, and pull the whole *control* thing again, but mercifully he kissed me and said, "I thought you'd never ask."

His pants were unbuckled and I was on his lap within seconds, the fabric of my dress pulled aside and the toy abandoned. The only thing I needed was him. Inside me.

The sex was hard and fast. I was so turned on, my release was almost immediate. As was his. And when it was over, I dropped my head to his shoulder and let him wrap his arms around me.

"You were right," I murmured into his ear.

"About what?"

"This was a birthday to remember. Thank you for making it so special."

He trailed a finger up my bare back. "But it's not over yet," he said.

I sat back in surprise, and shifted so I was off his lap. "What else could you possibly have in store?"

He didn't answer me right away, and instead pulled his clothing back into place. I hadn't even noticed the car was moving, so when the door opened and the driver offered me his hand to help me out, it took me a second to realize we were no longer in front of the restaurant.

We were on a hilltop—a cliff, really—that looked out over the town of Aspen Valley below. The lights of my hometown were beautiful. It had been years since I'd been up there and seen it from this angle.

Phillip wrapped his arms around me, and I leaned back into his embrace. "Do you remember the last time we were here?"

I nodded.

There'd only been one other time. "With you," I said. "We had a picnic under the stars with the lights below. I thought that night we might…" I trailed off. It didn't matter. It was in the past.

"I should have told you then that I loved you," he said. "I think I knew, even then, that I wanted to be with you forever. I never should have let you go."

I turned in his arms then. "We're past that now," I reminded him. "We're together now."

He nodded seriously. "And it's never too late."

I tilted my head in question, but it all became crystal-clear a moment later when he dropped to his knee and held out a ring. "Abigail, I love you with my entire heart. I always have."

My hand flew to my mouth and I swallowed back a sob.

"I made a mistake once, and I'll never make it again. These last few weeks, having you back in my life the way you should have always been, it has become clear to me that things are exactly how they should be. I don't want to spend one more moment without you as my wife. Will you, please, marry me?"

I'd already said yes a million times in my head, so it almost felt redundant when I finally managed a nod and a, "Yes. Of course." But when Phillip slipped the diamond ring on my left hand, the only thing I felt was happy.

He was right: things were exactly how they should be. He was mine, and I was his. Finally and forever.

***

**I hope you enjoyed Abby and Phillip's second chance at love that proves that taking a chance and pushing out of your comfort zone can pay off.
Join Phillip and Abby as they celebrate their first holiday together in a special bonus scene HERE**

What do you think? Would you take a chance and *just go for it?* Coming next, it's Jessie's turn. Will she take a risk and find love? Or instead will she lose everything, including her heart? Read on for a special sneak peek of Finally Mine.

And if you want even more romance…click HERE for an exclusive FREE novella that isn't available anywhere else!

Finally Mine

It's Jessie's turn to FINALLY find her Happily Ever After

I should have never agreed…

But it was only one ride….

Besides, I was *way* overdue for a little excitement.

A middle aged, overworked single mom barely keeping my head above water, I'm hardly living my best life.

He's a rough around the edges biker who can't be anything but trouble, and he's looking at me as if I'm the sexiest woman alive.

Maybe I shouldn't have said yes, but I needed a ride home. And he offered.

On two conditions:

1. Hold on.

2. Let go.

It was dangerous, but I was due for a little danger, and when he touched me…all bets were off. I would climb on the back of his bike every night for the rest of my life if he'd make me feel that way again.

And again.

He lights up every part of me.

Even my heart.

But I don't know anything about him. And when I find out...

Everything changes because I no longer know who or what to trust anymore.

And if I don't figure it out soon, I will lose everything.

Pre-Order Finally Mine Today!

Chapter One

It had been a long day. Correction. It had been *three* long days settling my twins, Sadie and Lucas, into their dorms three hours away. Fortunately, they'd chosen the same college, so I didn't have to figure out how to clone myself to be in two places at once. As it was, handling the move-out on my own, when their father bailed on the last minute with some feeble excuse about being *busy* that weekend, had been almost as much as I could handle.

Almost.

After ten years of dealing with Barrett's last-minute excuses, forgotten birthdays, and generally one disappointment after another, it was nothing we weren't used to. Sadly, I think the kids had come to expect it from him.

Not that it mattered. I'd handled it. Just the way I handled everything. I'd rented a truck and together we'd loaded up what felt like an unreasonable number of boxes and set off down the highway to their future.

After three days of climbing stairs and hauling boxes, every muscle in my forty-one-year-old body screamed for a hot bath and a glass of wine.

I gazed longingly at my tub, and the layer of dust in it. How long had it been since I'd actually sank into steamy bubbles? Had I *ever*?

Not for at least ten years.

There just wasn't time. Ever.

With a deep sigh, I peeled out of my worn jeans and T-shirt and hopped under the spray of the shower for a quick rinse before pulling a clean uniform out of the closet.

There was no other item in my wardrobe I wore more than the light-pink, thin cotton dress that was the uniform at Rosie's. As the owner of the little retro-style eatery on the edge of town, I probably could have chosen to wear whatever I wanted. But the customers didn't know that the chubby, middle-aged woman with her permanent ponytail that was starting to show a few lines of gray was anything more than the lady who poured their coffee and served them plates of burgers and fries. And they wouldn't care.

It was all about images. And the truck drivers, drunk college kids, and random travelers who frequented my diner wanted the experience of an *authentic* diner. So, day after day, and night after night, I stuffed my body into the dress.

I had to suck in a little bit to do up the dress. Eating nothing but takeout for the last few days probably hadn't done my already ample bosom any favors. The top button strained over my breasts. Having the twins when I was only twenty-three had changed my body in all kinds of ways I never would have imagined. Besides the stretch marks and thirty pounds I couldn't seem to shed, the most notable of those changes were the very large tits that made fitting into anything with actual buttons almost impossible. And that included my uniform.

I tried not to think about how quiet my house was as I

flipped off the lights and grabbed my purse. At the last minute, I picked up the paperback on my bedside table where it had sat, largely unread for the last few years. Maybe I'd have enough time to read now with the kids out of the house. I pushed away the aching loneliness that would only grow stronger and more insistent now that Sadie and Lucas were gone.

With a sigh, I looked at the book again and fanned the pages through my fingers. At the very least, maybe I could skip ahead to the sex scenes.

Reading about it was better than nothing.

But I knew I wouldn't read any of it, just as I knew that despite my best friends' urging me to, I wouldn't be having any sex. That would require me to put myself out there. And even with the kids gone now…there was no time.

And even if there was, I would hardly consider myself attractive to any of the eligible men in town—if there were any. I'd done nothing but work and raise my kids for as long as I could remember. The concept of having my hair done had fallen away years ago, leaving me with long, thick, almost unruly hair in desperate need of a date with scissors. I was softer and thicker, with much rounder curves than I would like and my makeup routine consisted of mascara and lip gloss—if I remembered.

I didn't consider myself *unattractive*, but compared to most of the women in Aspen Valley…well, there was no comparison.

Twenty minutes later, I rushed—late—through the door of Rosie's after dropping the rental truck off and taking the bus to the diner. I'd given the twins my car to share while they were at college, and selfishly, so they could come home for visits. But it meant I'd be taking public transit until I could find a minute and a few spare dollars to buy a new one.

"Doris, I'm so sorry that I'm late." I stashed my things behind the counter before straightening up to meet the unimpressed gaze of my longest employee.

It was almost impossible these days to find anyone willing to work for minimum wage plus tips, let alone a decent employee who would show up to their shifts and not steal. I needed Doris, and she knew it. But she and Stan, my longtime cook, were almost like family. I had no idea what I would do without them.

"I really owe you."

"You do." Her lips were pursed as she assessed me, the way she usually did. "But it was for the kiddos." She managed a small smile. Despite her tough, almost sour exterior, I knew how much she loved Sadie and Lucas. She and Stan had practically helped me raise them when I bought Rosie's ten years ago.

Doris had worked for the original Rosie, almost from the time they'd opened the diner many years earlier. She had opinions on how every aspect of the business should be run, down to and including how my uniform fit on any given day.

I held up one finger in warning when I saw her eagle eyes take in the state of my uniform. I knew my dress was too tight. It seemed as if all my dresses were too tight lately. The last thing I needed was her to tell me.

"Thank you very much for taking care of things while I was gone, Doris." I gave her a genuine smile, because despite how prickly she could be, I did really like the woman.

My smile must have softened her a little. "How are the kiddos? Did you get them settled okay?"

I nodded and bit my lip with the surge of sudden and completely unexpected tears rushing to my eyes.

I didn't cry. *Ever.* Not when my husband left me. Not when

my parents passed away shortly afterward in a car accident. Not when my kids moved out, leaving me alone.

Never.

Which was why the tear that slipped down my cheek took me completely off guard. I swiped it away and sniffed hard.

"Now, now." Doris patted my shoulder, her annoyance of a moment ago forgotten. "It's okay, Jessie. This is what's supposed to happen. You raise them up right and you send them off. It's the natural order of things. Not keep them home forever, living in your basement like so many your age seem to prefer. Young people need room to spread their wings. You did good."

It was probably Doris's uncharacteristic sensitivity that caused the next tear to slip out. And then the next. It wasn't until she grunted in response and headed into the kitchen to commiserate with Stan at the griddle that I was able to pull it together.

I must be sleep deprived. It was the only explanation for my emotions.

For the next hour, the diner was mercifully slow. Only in the sense that it allowed me to make a fresh pot of coffee and pull myself together. I didn't want to think about what the slower days and even slower nights meant for my bottom line.

Because no matter how I ran the numbers, they weren't good. Business was going down more and more every month. But the bills weren't. I hadn't missed the new Closed for Business signs in the windows of the neighboring shops. Every day, there were more of them popping up as the land developer got to them. There were only a few of us holdouts left. It was only a matter of time before Trent Thomas got what he wanted.

I'd tried to fight it and, dammit, I still wasn't ready to let go. And that's exactly what I'd tell him at our upcoming meeting. Although with every day that went by with fewer and fewer customers, I couldn't help but wonder what exactly it was that I was fighting for.

The bells over the door chimed, filling me with hope as the dinner rush, little as it might turn out to be, began.

\#

The bike vibrated beneath my legs as I pushed it faster and faster along the mountain road. Getting on my bike was my only fucking release these days. The only way I could leave the office behind and forget for a little while.

And I needed to forget.

At least for a few hours.

As the CEO of MultiTech Software, I was used to the pressures that came with business, but with the details of the latest takeover weighing heavily over my head, the stress was reaching a boiling point. Which was exactly why I'd broken out my Harley motorcycle.

The minute I ditched my suit jacket and Rolex and slid into my jeans and beat-up leathers, it was as though I could breathe again.

Nothing cleared my head like a long ride.

Except a good hard fuck.

My cock throbbed painfully, reminding me again of just how long it had been since I'd had that kind of release.

Why had it been so long?

I growled a little and shook my head as I pushed the bike faster.

I knew exactly why. The last woman whose company I'd enjoyed had recognized me. I couldn't have that. The last thing I needed was another fucking gold digger.

The moment any woman found out I was Shane Grant and, like so many in Aspen Valley, had more money than I could ever possibly spend in one lifetime, they very quickly made it their personal mission to help me with that spending.

I hated women like that.

Who only ever saw dollar signs when they looked at me. I was so much more than a fucking ATM card.

Using me for sex was one thing. That was an honest and equitable trade. I used her; she used me—perfect. But as soon as money got involved, it never failed: that same woman, who had been all about getting down and dirty, suddenly was more interested in a diamond ring.

No thanks.

Been there. Done that. One ex-wife was enough, thank you very much.

The yellow line of the highway passed in a blur as I drove hard and fast until finally, I was ready for a break. The neon lights of Rosie's on the edge of town beckoned to me. I'd lived in Aspen Valley for almost five years, and not once had I been to the out-of-the-way diner until a few days before when I'd stumbled upon it on a ride. And why would I have? Aspen Valley was full of the rich and the richer, and more uptight, fancy restaurants to cater to the wealthy than any other town I'd ever seen.

But the diner had a good cup of coffee, a decent piece of pie, and most importantly, no one I knew.

Chapter Two

By some sort of miracle, I had steady customers most of the night, the last table of four trailing out right before eleven. Perfect timing. My girlfriends were due for our weekly catch-up and drinks in a few minutes.

Once a week, no matter what was going on in our lives, we made a point to meet—mostly at the diner because I was inevitably working—and catch up with each other. We'd known each other since we were thirteen and no one knew me better. True family wasn't given to you by birthright, as far as I was concerned. It was the family you chose. My friends.

I wiped down the table and put on one last pot of coffee before the door opened, the bells announcing the arrival of Abby and Sandy.

"Hey."

I raised my hand in greeting, a smile on my face. I needed them more than I realized this week.

"Our usual booth?"

"You know it." I nodded. "Anyone need anything?"

Abby laughed and held up a martini shaker. "I brought mine."

I shook my head and laughed. The diner wasn't licensed, which meant it was probably a risky business move to let my friends bring their own alcohol in, but we'd been doing it so long, I hardly remembered I wasn't supposed to.

"I have a fresh pot of coffee on for you, Sandy."

She smiled her appreciation. I knew she'd have a little Tupperware container of Baileys to add to it. She always drank the same thing. Darla, when she arrived, late as usual, would have a flask of whiskey and unless it was a special occasion, Brittany would stick to soda water. Only very occasionally did she add a shot of vodka.

As for me, I kept a bottle of white wine in the back cooler. Before joining them, I poured myself a glass and had just re-emerged from the back when the bells over the door jingled again. I almost didn't look up, thinking it was Britt or Darla, but something about the air felt charged with the new arrival. I slid my glass out of sight and turned in time to see the customer head for a booth on the other side of the restaurant. "I'll be right with you," I called.

He lifted a finger in acknowledgment.

"Sorry, ladies," I apologized a moment later as I delivered a fresh cup of coffee for Sandy and empty glasses for Abby's martini and Darla's whiskey when she got there. "I'll just be a minute."

"Don't worry about it," Sandy said. She was the sweetest of all of us. There really was no other way to describe her besides sweet. "Don't rush on our account."

"That's right," Abby agreed as Darla arrived. "I was just going to tell you about—"

"Your latest sexy escapade?" Darla wiggled her eyebrows.

Abby smiled coyly, and we all laughed. It hadn't been long since Abby and her first true love, Phillip, had reconnected over a very indecent proposal that we'd encouraged her to accept that turned out to not only be super hot, but also a chance for the two of them to finally be together. Ever since, we'd been regaled with many tales of their very active sex life.

And I, for one, was more and more envious of my friend.

"Okay," I said. "Tell one story. But no more. Not without me." They nodded their agreement and I laughed. "I'll be back soon."

I hustled to the counter, grabbed a pot of coffee and a fresh cup, and headed over to where my new customer sat. I moved on autopilot, laughing to myself about what type of crazy antics Abby was going to tell us about next. I couldn't help it; I loved hearing about the amazing sex my friend was having. I might as well live vicariously through Abby. Lord knew I hadn't seen any action since my divorce—okay, longer than that. Barrett and I hadn't been intimate in a very, very long time before we finally called it quits on our marriage.

I was distracted, still thinking about my sex life—or, more accurately, lack thereof—and just going through the motions as I poured the coffee and slid it in front of my new customer. At least, that must have been the reason I hadn't noticed how fucking sexy the man was. Because the minute I looked...

"How are you to—" I damn near spilled the hot coffee on him as I caught a glimpse of eyes so gray, I had to take a second look to be sure they weren't silver.

"Careful there, sweetheart." He steadied the cup with his strong hands over mine. The simple touch sent a spark through me.

I pulled back quickly and tucked my free hand into my apron. He was older than me, but not by much, just enough that his dark hair was streaked with the slightest bit of silver. He wore head-to-toe leather, like he'd just climbed off a motor-cycle. I glanced out the picture window at the front of the restaurant and sure enough, parked under a light was a very shiny, very sexy bike.

I'd always had a bit of a fantasy about motorcycles.

The thought struck me sharply. I was *not* fantasizing about this man. *Was I?* Not after mere seconds of putting eyes on him.

I pulled myself back to the moment. "Sorry about that. I wasn't..."

I let the sentence drift away. *What was I supposed to say?* That I wasn't prepared for such a hot biker with thick biceps that my fingers were itching to squeeze, and those crazy piercing eyes, and the sexiest thick beard streaked with silver that matched his eyes to be sitting in my booth? I mean, I *could* say that. It was the truth.

"What can I get you?" I asked instead.

He smiled, but just a little, as if he knew what kind of effect he'd had on me and was enjoying every second of it. My body tingled under his attentions. How long had it been since I was flirted with? *Was* he flirting with me?

No. Not a man like this. Not with me.

"How about a little sugar?"

I stepped back. Flirting or not, that was way too forward. I shook my head, hard. There was *no* way I was going to give him any sugar. I don't care how sexy he was, or how long it had been, or how damp my panties were just from being in his presence. *There was no way I was going to—*

"Sugar?" He pointed to the table behind me and the sugar shaker.

Oh. Right.

I turned to grab it, taking the opportunity to exhale. I placed the sugar in front of him with a little more force than necessary.

"You didn't think I meant something else, did you?" He lifted his eyebrow, and I knew my face burned red. I could feel the flush all the way down my chest.

Behind me, I heard the bells over the door jingle, followed by Brittany and Darla's voices, but the sexy biker's gaze didn't leave me. I took a breath and regrouped. "What would you like?"

"Now look who's being forward." He wiggled his eyebrows this time, but his eyes still didn't leave mine. They held me. Almost hypnotizing me. It was ridiculous, but I couldn't look away. And I wasn't sure I wanted to.

"I'm not...I wasn't..."

"Why don't we wait until we know each other a little better, sweetheart."

My face blazed even hotter, and I shifted where I stood because something about this stranger made me feel things I hadn't felt in a very long time.

His eyes traveled down my body.

Was it my imagination or did his pupils darken when he got to my chest?

Once more his gaze moved up and locked on mine. "It's nice to meet you, Jessie." He stuck out his hand, and I had to put the coffeepot down to take it. His grip was strong, and instantly, images of what his hands would feel like pressed up on other parts of my body flashed through my head.

"How did you know my..." I pulled my hand away as if I'd been bit. *This was too much.*

He chuckled and pointed to my chest, where my name tag was pinned.

I glanced at it briefly, as if double-checking to make sure it was still there, and all I could see was my breasts, straining and —*oh my God*—heaving, against the cheap fabric of my pink uniform dress. "Oh."

"Just the coffee for me, Jessie."

I nodded, but my face flared hot again when he added, "For now."

#

Just like every other night for the last few nights I'd gone riding, I'd only been looking for a cup of coffee.

Not a hard-on so intense I thought it might cause personal injury if I didn't stop looking at the curvy waitress in the pale-pink dress stretched tight across her tits in all the right ways.

Damn.

I knew I was in trouble the moment I walked in and saw her, and her heavy breasts popping from the top of her uniform as she leaned over the counter.

The last fucking thing I needed was a sexy piece of ass distracting me.

Or maybe that was the very thing I *did* need.

She was the exact opposite of the women I usually dated— or more specifically, screwed. And it had been a long time since I'd indulged in a little distraction of that nature. And Lord knew I was well overdue.

But this woman...

I lifted my mug and took a sip of the strong, bitter coffee before I poured another dose of sugar in. She might look pretty fucking good in her uniform, but her coffee-making skills needed a little work.

My eyes drifted back to the counter where she busied herself for a moment with something under the counter—*was that a glass of wine?*—before joining a group of women crowded mostly out of sight in the back corner booth.

I sipped slowly as I watched her.

She was older than the young, giggling, almost absurd girls I usually hooked up with. Jessie was a woman. She looked like a hard worker. A little tired, but not worn out. Almost determined. As if life was a challenge she was determined to conquer.

Why hadn't I seen her before?

I chuckled into my mug. I'd only been visiting the diner for exactly three days. It's not as if I knew anything about the place or the staff. And I knew nothing about this woman who was currently laughing with the group of women in the corner instead of checking on her customer. A quick glance around the place told me I was the only one. *Still, should she be sitting down on the job?* Not likely. And I was almost positive that was wine she'd taken with her.

Not that I'd rat her out. That wasn't my style.

But it *was* my style to press her up against the—

No. She wasn't my type. And Jessie didn't seem like the type of woman who'd bend so easily. She'd be a challenge.

Maybe that's exactly what I needed?

There was nothing like the thrill of the chase, followed by the conquest, that released the pressure quite the same way.

Hands on those full hips while I bent her over and relieved that building pressure. *Oh yes, I could picture exactly how—*

"Can I get you anything else?"

I'd been so busy imagining what it would be like to have her that I hadn't noticed Jessie approach, coffeepot in hand.

"A piece of pie, maybe? It's delicious."

"I'm sure it is." I didn't bother telling her I'd enjoyed a piece of pie every other night.

"Stan makes it himself." She gestured behind her toward the kitchen, where the stereotypically bald, with a potbelly, cook stood over a grill. "It's peach."

I knew from experience exactly how good the pie was. But there was only one kind of sweet I wanted at the moment.

"Just some more coffee."

"It's not too strong, is it?" It was, but I didn't say anything as she topped up my cup. "I made it really strong tonight because my friend usually adds—"

She cut herself off before she could incriminate herself.

Too late.

"Does she add some cream liqueur?" I nodded toward the table of women, two of whom were doing a terrible job of pretending not to watch us.

Jessie's mouth opened in an O.

Before she could protest, I added, "I didn't know you served alcohol here."

"We don't."

"Is that right?" I smirked and bit my bottom lip a little as I assessed her. "And I suppose that wasn't a glass of wine you poured yourself behind the counter."

Again, her mouth fell open, but only for a minute before she clamped it shut again and pressed her lips in a line.

"I wonder how your boss would feel to hear that you're—"

Just like that, her face shifted, so she was now the one with the grin. "I *am* the boss." She jutted out a full hip and shot me a satisfied look.

Now *that* was an unexpected twist.

"Is that right?"

"Surprised?"

I was. But it explained a lot. And left a lot more questions at the same time.

"It's pretty quiet in here." I dodged the question.

Her face fell, the grin slipping away. She sighed. "It never used to be. But…it doesn't matter."

Her eyes betrayed her words. I could see exactly how much it mattered. She was worried about the business slowdown.

I shifted in my seat in an effort to release the pressure in my pants that had only grown worse the longer she stood there. "Maybe I'll have that piece of pie after all."

She laughed a little, a sweet sound. But she shook her head. "You don't need to buy pity pie. It's fine."

"It's not fine." I reached for my coffee cup to keep from reaching for her. "Besides, I know just how delicious it is." I gave myself away. "I've been in every night all week." No point in keeping it a secret. "I haven't seen you before."

More than anything, I wanted to keep her talking. Her attention on me.

She put the pot down on the table. "That's because I was delivering my twins to college."

Twins? College?

My eyes went to her left hand in search of a ring. It wasn't something I usually cared about.

Usually.

No ring.

Once more, I met her eyes. "That would explain the absence."

She stretched her arms behind her back in a way that thrust her tits forward. My gaze homed in on the button that looked as though it only just barely held the thin fabric over her chest closed. I willed the button to let go.

It held.

"My first absence in almost ten years." She rolled her

shoulders. "Too bad it wasn't much of a vacation. Driving a truck and lugging boxes isn't my idea of a break."

So, she'd done it alone.

"Speaking of which," she continued, almost talking to herself. "I suppose I better start looking for a new car."

"Car?"

She blinked, as if she just realized she was speaking aloud.

"You said you needed to look for a new car," I prompted.

"Oh, that." She waved her hand in the air. "It's just that I rented a truck to move the kids out and I left them my car to share while they got settled. But it's just an old...well, it doesn't matter. But I was going to surprise them with it and get something...sorry. I'm rambling."

She was. I liked it. She was off-balance around me. I *really* liked that.

"Anyway." She took a breath and smiled brightly. "I guess there's no rest for the wicked."

I was grateful to be sitting down, because there was no way I would've been able to hide how hard that comment made my dick. *Wicked. I bet.*

And I'd certainly like to find out for myself. Not only that, but I'd also like to give this curvy beauty exactly the kind of break she deserved.

She rolled her shoulders back once more and picked up the coffeepot. "I'll go get you that piece of pie." She paused and assessed me. "If you really want it, that is?"

I swallowed hard. "Oh, I want it."

Pre-Order Finally Mine now!

About the Author

Elena Aitken is a USA Today Bestselling Author of more than fifty romance and women's fiction novels. The mother of 'grown up' twins, Elena now lives with her very own mountain man in the heart of the very mountains she writes about. She can often be found with her toes in the lake and a glass of wine in her hand, dreaming up her next book and working on her own happily ever after.

To learn more about Elena:
www.elenaaitken.com
elena@elenaaitken.com

www.ingramcontent.com/pod-product-compliance
Lightning Source LLC
Chambersburg PA
CBHW030343180626
46812CB00007B/2743